The President's Hat

The President's Hat

The President's Hat

Antoine Laurain

Translated from the French by Gallic Books

Gallic Books
London

This book is supported by the Institut français du Royaume-Uni
as part of the Burgess programme.

www.frenchbooknews.com

A Gallic Book

First published in France as *Le Chapeau de Mitterrand* by Flammarion, 2012
Copyright © Flammarion, Paris, 2012
English translation copyright © Gallic Books, 2013

First published in Great Britain in 2013 by Gallic Books,
59 Ebury Street, London, SW1W 0NZ

A CIP record for this book is available from the British Library
ISBN 978-1-908313-47-8

Typeset in Fournier MT by Gallic Books
Printed in the UK by CPI (CR0 4YY)

2 4 6 8 10 9 7 5 3

Wearing a hat confers undeniable authority over those without one.
Tristan Bernard

Daniel Mercier went up the stairs at Gare Saint-Lazare as the crowd surged down. Men and women hurried distractedly past him, most clutching briefcases but some with suitcases. In the crush, they could easily have knocked into him but they didn't. On the contrary, it seemed as though they parted to let him through. At the top of the steps, he crossed the main concourse and headed for the platforms. Here too it was crowded, with an uninterrupted tide of humanity pouring from the trains. Daniel forced his way through to the arrivals board. The train would be arriving at platform 23. He retraced his steps and stood next to the ticket-punching machines.

At 9.45 p.m. train 78654 ground into the station and released its passengers. Daniel craned his neck, looking for his wife and son. He saw Véronique first. She waved, then described a circle above her head, finishing her gesture with an astonished look. Jérôme meanwhile made a bee-line for his father, flinging himself at his legs and almost tripping him up. When Véronique reached them, slightly out of breath, she stared at her husband.

'What on earth is that hat?'

'It's Mitterrand's hat.'

'I can see it's Mitterrand's hat.'

'No,' Daniel corrected her. 'I mean this really is Mitterrand's hat.'

When he'd told her at the station that it really was Mitterrand's hat, Véronique had stared at him again, her head on one side, with that little frown she always wore when she was trying to work out if he was having her on or not. The same frown as when Daniel had asked her to marry him, or when he'd first asked her out on a date to an exhibition at the Beaubourg. In other words, the frown that was the reason, amongst others, that he had fallen in love with her.

'What do you mean?' she had asked incredulously.

'Have you got Mitterrand's hat, Papa?'

'Yes I have,' Daniel had replied, grabbing their bags.

'So you're the president?'

'Yep, that's me. President of the Republic,' Daniel had answered, delighted by his son's suggestion.

Daniel had refused to divulge anything further as they drove back.

'I'll tell you all about it when we get home.'

Véronique had pressed him, but he stood firm. When they got up to their sixteenth-floor apartment in the fifteenth *arrondissement*, Daniel announced that he'd made supper. Cold meat, chicken, tomato and basil salad, and cheese. Véronique was impressed – her husband rarely made dinner. First they had an aperitif.

'Take a seat,' said Daniel, who had still not taken off his hat.

Véronique sat. And Jérôme snuggled up beside her.

'To us,' said Daniel, solemnly clinking glasses with his wife.

Jérôme copied them with his Orangina.

Daniel removed his hat and held it out to Véronique. She took it carefully, running her finger over the felt. Jérôme immediately did the same.

'Are your hands clean?' his mother asked anxiously.

Then she turned the hat upside down, and her eye fell on the band of leather running round the inside. The two gold letters stood out clearly: F.M. Véronique looked up at her husband.

The evening before, Daniel had stopped his Golf at the junction. He'd turned off the radio, cutting off Caroline Loeb as she droned on about liking cotton wool. The hit song with its slow, insistent refrain was now stuck in his head. He had massaged his aching shoulder, trying unsuccessfully to get the crick out of his neck. He hadn't heard from his wife and son, who were in Normandy with his parents-in-law for the holidays. Perhaps there would be a message on the answering machine when he got home. The tape was starting to wear out and hadn't been rewinding properly for the last few days. He really should buy a new machine. How did people manage before answering machines? wondered Daniel. The telephone rang and rang, no one answered it, and then they rang back later, that's how.

The idea of shopping on his own then making supper for himself in the silent flat was unbearable. He had started fantasising about going to a restaurant – a really good brasserie, perhaps – at about four o'clock that afternoon as he was checking the last of the expenses slips submitted by the SOGETEC auditors. He hadn't been to a really good brasserie for at least a year. The last time had been with Véronique and Jérôme. His son, only six at the time, had been very well-behaved. They had ordered the seafood platter royale, a bottle of Pouilly-Fuissé, and a hamburger with mashed potato for Jérôme, who had declared, to his father's great disappointment, that he didn't want to try the oysters.

'Not even one?'

'No,' said Jérôme, shaking his head.

Véronique had defended her son. 'He's got plenty of time.'

It was true. Jérôme had plenty of time.

It was eight o'clock now, and the early-winter cold was already gripping the city, muffling its sounds and the noise of the passing traffic. He had driven past this particular brasserie several times before. Now as he drove tentatively from the boulevard to the next street, he finally spotted it. That was definitely the one, with its big red awning, oyster bar outside, and waiters in spotless white aprons.

A meal all on his own, with no wife and no child, awaited him inside. The sort of meal he used to enjoy occasionally before he was married. Back then his salary hadn't stretched to anywhere as smart as this. But even in the modest establishments he'd frequented, he had always eaten well and never felt the need of company as he savoured *andouillette*, a decent cut of beef, or a dish of whelks. The fading light held the promise of a bachelor evening. What a pleasing phrase.

'A bachelor evening,' he repeated, slamming the door of the Golf.

Daniel was experiencing the need 'to find himself,' as one of the guests had said on a recent programme on Antenne 2. The guest was a psychotherapist who'd written a book about stress at work and was on the programme to promote it. Daniel found the concept appealing. This gourmet interlude would allow him to get back in touch with his true self, to throw off the stress of the day, and to forget about accounts and figures and the recent tensions caused by the reorganisation of the finance department.

Jean Maltard had taken over as director, and Daniel, who was deputy director, couldn't see anything good about the appointment. Nothing good at all, not for the department as a whole, nor for him personally. Crossing the boulevard, he was determined to put his worries right out of his mind. As soon as I open the brasserie door, he told himself, there will be no more Jean Maltard, no more SOGETEC, no more expenses slips, no more VAT. Just me and a seafood platter royale.

The white-aproned waiter had walked ahead of him down the line of tables where couples, families and tourists sat chatting, smiling or nodding their heads, their mouths full. Along the way, he spotted seafood platters, entrecôte steaks with *pommes vapeur*, *faux-filets* with Béarnaise sauce.

When he had first entered, the head waiter, a rotund man with a slender moustache, had enquired whether he had booked. For a moment, Daniel thought his evening was over.

'I didn't have time,' he answered tonelessly.

The head waiter had raised an eyebrow and peered closely at the evening's list of reservations.

A young blonde woman came over. 'Twelve called to cancel half an hour ago,' she said, pointing to a name on the list.

'And no one thought to tell me?' The head waiter was visibly annoyed.

'I thought Françoise had told you,' the girl said offhandedly, wandering off.

The maître d' had closed his eyes for a moment, his pained expression suggesting the full extent of the self-control required not to explode with fury at the waitress's blunder.

'Allow us to show you to your table, Monsieur,' he said to Daniel, nodding to a waiter, who immediately hurried over.

All brasseries have brilliant white tablecloths that hurt the eyes, like snow on the ski slopes. The glasses and the silverware really do sparkle. For Daniel, the characteristic glitter of tableware in the best brasseries was the embodiment of luxury. The waiter returned with the menu and the wine list. Daniel opened the red leatherette folder and began to read. The prices were much higher than he had imagined, but he decided not to worry about that. The *plateau royal de fruits de mer* was framed in the middle of the page, in elegant calligraphy: *fines de claire creuses et plates de Bretagne*, half a crab, three different kinds of clam, prawns, langoustines, whelks, shrimps, cockles and winkles.

Daniel took the wine list and looked for a Pouilly-Fuissé or -Fumé. This, too, was more expensive than he had anticipated. Daniel ordered his platter, adding a half-bottle of Pouilly-Fuissé.

'I'm afraid we only have bottles,' said the waiter.

Daniel didn't want to appear miserly. 'A bottle will be fine,' he said, closing the wine list.

Couples, on the whole. Tables of men in ties and grey suits like his own, except that theirs were clearly the best designer labels. They might even have been made to measure. The four fifty-somethings seated a little further down must be celebrating the end of a tough day and the signature of a decent contract. The quartet sipped at glasses of no doubt excellent wine. They each wore the calm, confident smile of a man who has succeeded in life. At another table beneath the large mirrors, an elegant brunette in a red dress was listening to a grey-haired man who Daniel could see only from the back. She was half listening, in fact; from time to time her gaze wandered around the room, before returning to the speaker opposite her. She looked bored.

The wine waiter brought a silver ice bucket on a stand, the bottle of Pouilly bobbing amongst the ice cubes. The waiter took hold of the corkscrew and performed the ritual opening, passing the cork under his nose. Daniel tasted the wine, which seemed good to him. He was not one of those wine buffs who can distinguish every last nuance of flavour in a fine cru and discourse on it at length, in sophisticated terms. The wine waiter, in time-honoured fashion, awaited his customer's opinion with an air of vague condescension. Daniel gave an approving nod designed to indicate great erudition on the subject of white Burgundy. The wine waiter gave a small smile, filled his glass and departed.

A few moments later, a waiter placed a round stand in the middle of the table, a sign that the seafood platter was about to arrive. Next came a basket of pumpernickel bread, a ramekin of shallot vinegar, and the butter dish. Daniel buttered a piece of bread and dipped it discreetly in the mixture – a ritual he performed every time he ate a seafood platter in a restaurant. The taste of the vinegar was chased away by a mouthful of chilled wine. He gave a satisfied sigh. Yes, he had found himself.

The platter arrived, the seafood arranged by species on a bed of crushed ice. Daniel took an oyster, held a quarter of lemon immediately above it, and squeezed gently. A drop of lemon juice fell onto the delicate membrane, which squirmed immediately. Absorbed by the oyster's iridescent gleam, he nevertheless noticed the next-door table being moved to one side. Looking up, he saw the moustachioed head waiter smiling at a new customer. A man who removed his red scarf, then his coat and hat and slipped onto the banquette beside Daniel.

'May I hang those up for you?' asked the maître d' immediately.

'No, no. I'll just leave them here on the banquette. If they're not bothering you, Monsieur?'

'No,' said Daniel in a barely audible voice. 'Not at all,' he added in a whisper.

François Mitterrand had just sat down next to him.

Two men sat down opposite the head of state. One was large and stocky with glasses and curly hair, the other slender, with grey hair swept back in an elegant wave. The latter bestowed a brief, benevolent smile on Daniel, who summoned what remained of his composure and attempted to smile back. He recognised that face with its piercing eyes and narrow lips. And then he remembered who it was. It was Roland Dumas, who had been the Foreign Minister. Dumas had handed over to a successor when the Socialist Party had lost its parliamentary majority eight months ago.

I am dining next to the President of the Republic, Daniel kept repeating to himself, trying to convince himself that, irrational as it might seem, it was really happening to him. He barely noticed the taste of his first oyster, so preoccupied was he by his new neighbour. The strangeness of the situation made him feel as if he might wake up any moment at home in bed and find that it was all a dream. Around the restaurant, other diners were pretending not to gaze in the general direction of the table next to Daniel's.

As he picked up his second oyster he glanced discreetly to his left. The President had put on his glasses and was reading the menu. Daniel took in the famous noble profile, seen in magazines, on television and every New Year's Eve for the past five years. Now he was seeing that profile in the flesh. He could have put out a hand and touched François Mitterrand.

The waiter returned and the President ordered a dozen oysters, and the salmon. The large man chose mushroom pâté and a rare steak, while Roland Dumas followed the President's lead with oysters and fish. A few minutes later, the wine waiter appeared with a silver ice bucket on a stand containing another bottle of Pouilly-Fuissé bathed in ice. He uncorked the bottle smoothly and poured a little into the presidential glass. François Mitterrand tasted it, approving it with a brief nod.

Daniel poured himself another glass of wine, and drank it down almost in one, before taking a teaspoon of the red shallot vinegar and dressing an oyster.

'As I was saying to Helmut Kohl last week ...' Daniel heard François Mitterrand say as he ate his oyster. Never again, he told himself, would he be able to eat oysters with vinegar without hearing those words: 'As I was saying to Helmut Kohl last week'.

A waiter placed a small carafe of red in front of the large bespectacled man who immediately poured himself a glass, as another waiter brought the starters. The fat man tasted the pâté, which he said was good, and launched into a story about wild mushroom terrine. The President swallowed an oyster while Daniel removed a pin from the cork covered in silver paper, ready to make a start on the winkles.

'Michel has some wonderful wines in his cellar,' confided Roland Dumas, with a knowing air.

The President looked up at him, and Michel continued with an account of his cellar in the country, where he also kept cigars from all over the world, and dried *saucisson*. He was as proud of his *saucissons* as he was of his cigars.

'How original, to collect *saucissons*!' said François Mitterrand, squeezing his lemon.

Daniel swallowed his tenth winkle and glanced once more to his left. The President had finished his last oyster and was wiping his mouth with the spotless white napkin.

'Before I forget,' he began, addressing Roland Dumas, 'our friend's telephone number …'

'Yes, of course,' murmured Dumas, reaching into his jacket pocket.

The President turned to his coat, picked up his hat and placed it behind the brass bar that ran around the top of the banquette. He took a leather notebook from his coat pocket, put his glasses back on and leafed through the pages.

'The last name at the bottom,' he said, handing the notebook to Dumas, who took it, silently copied the name and number into his own diary, then passed the book back to François Mitterrand, who put it back in his coat pocket.

Michel began another anecdote about a man whose name meant nothing to Daniel. Dumas looked as if he was enjoying the story and François Mitterrand smiled, saying, 'That's a bit harsh,' but he said it jokingly, encouraging the speaker to continue.

'I assure you it's true, I was there!' the large man insisted, spreading the last of his pâté on a piece of bread.

Daniel listened to the story. He felt as if he were sitting in on a private, rather risqué gathering. The other diners in the brasserie counted for nothing. It was only the four of them now.

'And what about you, Daniel, what do you think?'

Daniel would have turned to the head of state, and uttered things of great interest to François Mitterrand. The President would have nodded in agreement, and then Daniel would have turned to Roland Dumas and asked his opinion. Dumas would have nodded, too, and Michel would have added enthusiastically, 'I agree with Daniel!'

'That woman is remarkably beautiful,' said François Mitterrand, quietly.

Daniel followed his gaze. The President was looking at the brunette in the red dress. Dumas took advantage of the arrival of the main courses to turn round discreetly. The large man did the same.

'A very beautiful woman,' he concurred.

'I agree,' murmured Dumas.

Daniel felt a sense of communion with the head of state. François Mitterrand had ordered the same wine as him, and now he had spotted the same woman. It was quite something to have the same tastes as the First Frenchman. Indeed, the convivial exchange of half-expressed appreciations of womenkind had cemented many a masculine friendship, and Daniel fell to daydreaming he was the fourth man at the President's table. He too had a black leather diary from which the former Foreign Minister would be delighted to copy out contacts. The fat man's cellar held no secrets for him, indeed he visited it regularly, savouring *saucisson* and lighting up the finest Havana cigars the world had ever seen. And of course, he accompanied the President on his Parisian walks, along the quaysides of the Seine, past the *bouquinistes'* stalls, both of them with their hands clasped behind their backs, discoursing on the way of the world, or simply admiring the sunset from the Pont des Arts. Passers-by would turn back to look at their familiar silhouettes, and people he knew would murmur, *sotto voce*, 'Oh yes, Daniel knows François Mitterrand very well ...'

'Is everything all right?'

The waiter's voice interrupted Daniel's reverie. Yes, everything was very good indeed. He would make his seafood platter last as long as was necessary. Even if he had to stay until closing time, he would not get up from his seat on the banquette before the President left. He was doing it for himself, and for others, so that one day he would be able to say: 'I dined beside François Mitterrand in a brasserie in November 1986. He was right next to me, this close. I could see him as clearly as I can see you now.' In his mind, Daniel was already rehearsing the words he would use in the decades to come.

Two hours and seven minutes had gone by. François Mitterrand had just disappeared into the night, flanked by Dumas and the large man, after the maître d' had ceremoniously held the door for them. All three had finished their meal with a crème brûlée. The large man had removed a cigar from a leather case, telling them he would light it outside and smoke it while they walked. Dumas had paid with a 500-franc note.

'Shall we?' the President had asked.

Dumas had got to his feet. The cloakroom attendant had appeared and helped him on with his coat. She had done the same for Michel, who had complained he could still feel his lumbago, but the President had put on his own coat, and then his red scarf. As he did this he had turned towards the brunette and their eyes had met. She had smiled, very slightly, and the President had doubtless responded in kind, but Daniel had not been able to see that. All three had then headed for the door. In the restaurant, everyone had leant towards their fellow diners and conversations were quieter for a few seconds.

Voilà. It was over.

Nothing remained but the empty plates, the cutlery, the glasses and the barely crumpled white napkins. Now it was just a table like any other, thought Daniel. In a few minutes, the dishes would be cleared away, the tablecloth refreshed, and a new diner would settle himself onto the banquette for the second sitting, never suspecting that the President of the Republic had occupied the very same seat less than an hour earlier.

Daniel had kept back one last, slightly milky oyster, which had been waiting its turn on the melting ice for the last twenty minutes at least. He tipped a teaspoon of red-wine vinegar over it and tasted it. The iodine spread across his tongue, mixed with the bitter, peppery vinegar: 'As I was saying to Helmut Kohl last week ...' He was certain now – he would remember those words for the rest of his life.

Daniel swallowed his last mouthful of Pouilly and put his glass back down on the table. The dinner had been unreal – and he could so easily have missed it. He could have decided to go home and make his own supper, he could have chosen a different brasserie, there might not have been a free table, the customer who'd booked the table might not have cancelled ... The important events in our lives are always the result of a sequence of tiny details. The thought made him feel slightly dizzy – or was it the fact that he'd drunk a whole bottle of Pouilly-Fuissé?

He closed his eyes for a few seconds, breathed deeply,

shifted his shoulder and massaged his neck. As he raised his left hand to do this, Daniel touched the brass rail at the top of the banquette. His fingers encountered the cold metal, and then something else as well. Something soft and yielding, something that had just squirmed, like the oyster. Daniel turned to look: the hat was still there. Instinctively, he glanced over to the door of the brasserie. The President had left several minutes ago. There was no one in the doorway.

François Mitterrand had forgotten his hat. The phrase took shape in his mind. This is François Mitterrand's hat. Here, right next to you. Proof that this evening was real; absolute proof that it had really happened. Daniel turned to look again at the hat which had been carefully placed between the brass rail and the mirror. Behind the black hat, the whole restaurant was reflected.

Instead of calling over the head waiter to say self-importantly, 'I think the customer at the table next to me has left his hat behind,' and receiving obsequious thanks, Daniel acted on impulse. He felt as if he had a double and that another Daniel Mercier now stood in the middle of the dining room, witness to the simple, irreversible action that would be taken in the next few seconds. Daniel watched as he raised his own hand to the brass bar, lifted the black hat carefully by the brim and slipped it onto his lap, where it remained hidden from view under the table.

The whole operation took no more than three and a half seconds, but it seemed to him to have been performed in desperately slow motion, so that when the sounds of the dining room reached his ears once more, he felt as if he was emerging from a long period underwater. The blood beat in his temples and his heart thumped in his chest. What if someone came back to claim the hat now, he thought, in a brief moment of panic. A bodyguard? The President himself? What would he do? What could he possibly say? How could he explain the sudden transfer of the hat to his lap?

He had just committed an act of theft. The last time he had stolen something was in early adolescence, in a shopping centre in Courbevoie, egged on by a friend after school. They had stolen a record: 'Aline', a hit single by the pop star Christophe. Since that afternoon back in 1965, he had never done such a thing again.

What he had just done was far worse than sneaking a record into his schoolbag in a supermarket. Daniel sat motionless, his eyes darting around the room at the other diners. No, no one had seen him, he was sure of that. Nothing to fear on that score. But now he had to leave before anything untoward happened, before the President asked someone to call the restaurant, looking for his hat; before the waiters came scurrying to the table under the furious gaze of the maître d'.

Daniel asked for the bill, saying he would pay by card. The waiter returned with the credit card machine. Daniel hardly noticed the amount. Nothing mattered any more. He signed the slip and took his receipt. He rummaged in his pockets for a tip and put it in the chrome dish. The waiter bowed slightly in a gesture of thanks and walked away.

Now, said Daniel to himself. His mouth was dry so he

poured himself a glass of water and gulped it down, then delicately extracted the presidential hat from under the tablecloth and put it on his head. Yes, it fitted perfectly. He put on his coat and headed for the door, feeling as if his legs were about to give way. The maître d' would stop him: '*Pardonnez-moi, Monsieur! S'il vous plaît!* The hat, Monsieur ...?'

But nothing of the kind happened. Daniel had left a fifteen-franc tip, and the waiters all nodded respectfully as he passed; even the maître d' attempted a smile which lifted the tips of his narrow moustache. The door was held open for him, and he stepped out into the cold, turning up the collar of his coat and heading for his car. Mitterrand's hat is on my head, he told himself.

Once in the driver's seat, with the hat still on his head, Daniel angled the rear-view mirror and gazed at his reflection in silence for several minutes. He felt as if his brain was bathed in a refreshing dose of sparkling aspirin. Bubbles of oxygen were fizzing through zones that had slumbered for too long. He turned the key in the ignition and drove off slowly into the night.

Daniel drove through the streets for a long while, circling his neighbourhood several times before leaving the car on level five of his building's underground car park. He could have driven like that for hours, his mind a complete blank. He felt buoyed up with a confidence that was as comforting as a warm bath.

In the deserted living room, he sat down on the sofa and looked at his reflection in the blank television screen. He saw a man sitting with a hat on his head, nodding slowly. He stayed like that for a good hour, contemplating his own image, his entire being suffused with an almost mystical feeling of serene calm. It was two in the morning before he listened to his wife's message on the answering machine. Everything was fine in Normandy, Véronique and Jérôme would be back next day, arriving at Gare Saint-Lazare at 9.45 p.m. Daniel undressed. The last item he removed was the hat. He gazed in wonder at two letters embossed in gold on the band of leather running round the inside:

F.M.

In his account of the evening, Daniel allowed himself just one slight alteration – the seafood platter now featured no more than twenty-four oysters, half a crab and a few winkles. He knew that if he gave the full details of his sumptuous dinner, there was a danger Véronique would concentrate solely on the expense. Comments like 'Well, you certainly look after yourself when we're not around,' or 'I see, dining in solitary splendour!' would interfere with the re-telling of his adventure. In Daniel's version of the story, the arrival of the head of state assumed near-biblical proportions, and the phrase accompanying the vinegared oysters, 'As I was saying to Helmut Kohl last week', rang out like a divine commandment from the cavernous halls of heaven.

'Still, I'm shocked.'

'Shocked? Why?' said Daniel.

'That you stole the hat. It's not like you.'

'I didn't steal it as such,' he objected, irritated, although much the same thought had occurred to him as well. 'Let's just say I didn't give it back.'

Véronique seemed to accept that. He managed to convince her that he had, in fact, done the right thing by holding on to the hat because the moustachioed maître d' would probably have kept it for himself. Worse, if he hadn't spotted it, another customer might have taken it, unaware of the identity of its illustrious owner.

When they'd finished supper and Jérôme had gone to bed, they returned to the sitting room. Véronique carefully picked up the felt hat and sat stroking it, as if seized by a sudden melancholy. She regretted that Daniel hadn't been quicker to spot that François Mitterrand had left it behind: he could have called after the President and given it back to him with a smile.

'There would have been an understanding between you,' she remarked, sadly.

'Yes, but he was too far away,' Daniel pointed out. He still preferred the real-life version of the story, the one that ended with him wearing the presidential hat on his own head.

'I don't share your point of view at all, Monsieur Maltard,' said Daniel, shaking his head. He touched the hat that he'd placed in front of him on the big conference-room table.

Jean Maltard and the ten other members of the finance department summoned to the eleven o'clock meeting stared at him dumbfounded. Daniel allowed a few moments of silence to pass, a sphinx-like smile playing on his lips, then heard himself refute, point for point, the arguments put forward by the new departmental director.

With unprecedented confidence, he watched himself negotiate the complex layers of diplomacy with the ease of a dolphin leaping through the waves. When he had finished stating his case, a great silence fell upon the room. Bernard Falgou stared at him open-mouthed. Michèle Carnavan ventured a small cough, then, despairing of her spineless male colleagues, spoke out.

'I think Daniel has summarised our concerns perfectly.'

'Brilliantly,' added Bernard Falgou quickly, as if prodded by a tiny electric shock.

Maltard gazed impassively at Daniel. 'Nice work, Monsieur Mercier,' he announced icily.

Jean-Bernard Desmoine, head of Finance, had travelled up specially to attend the meeting, called to put the finishing touches to SOGETEC's new objectives for the Paris-Nord section. He kept his eyes fixed on Daniel as he made his case, scribbling a few brief notes when he explained with perfect clarity, and the figures to back him up, that they couldn't sensibly split the department into three divisions, but two at the very most.

'Thank you for coming, everyone,' said Jean-Bernard Desmoine. 'I'll let you get back to your desks. I'd like a word, Monsieur Maltard.'

Maltard agreed with a meek, insincere smile, then glared at Daniel. Only Bernard Falgou caught the look of cold hatred directed at his subordinate by the new departmental director. As soon as they had left the conference room, Falgou took Daniel by the arm.

'You slaughtered him, you slaughtered Maltard!' he said.

'Not really,' protested Daniel, blinking.

'But you did!' insisted Françoise. 'He's out on his ear, no doubt about it. That's what Desmoine's telling him right now. You demolished every one of his arguments.'

They gathered round him, excited to discover in their colleague a man of quiet strength, capable of defending their interests better than the most radical union representative, the best, most articulate lawyer. They praised his calm demeanour, his air of assurance, the extraordinary way he had of saying the unpalatable with the utmost tact.

'True class,' said Michèle Carnavan.

*

Back in his office, Daniel settled into his swivel chair, stroked his hat, which he had placed on the desk in front of him, and savoured the quiet of the room. He closed his eyes. He had got through the meeting without being assailed by one of the waves of anxiety that had plagued him since early childhood. On the contrary, he had experienced a sense of serene calm. Just a few days ago, the very idea of a confrontation with Jean Maltard would have raised his blood pressure and brought on an attack of heartburn with the last bite of lunch. Tense as a bowstring, he would have played back their exchange over and over again in his mind, castigating himself all afternoon for some clumsy phrase, some word or point that had, unquestionably, caused him to hand the argument to Maltard. Daniel would have emerged ashen and drained at the end of the day.

Not so now. He felt fine, as one might at the seaside, walking in the sand, late on a summer's afternoon. This new state of affairs came as no great surprise. It was as if the real Daniel Mercier had finally stepped out into the light of day. The earlier model was just some unfinished prototype, a work in progress. He raised the Venetian blind on his office window, letting the winter sunshine stream in, and immersed himself in his SOGETEC files once more.

It was well past seven o'clock when Jean Maltard pushed open his deputy's glass door, without knocking.

'Staying the night?' he asked drily. 'There's no overtime for deputy departmental managers ...'

34

Daniel looked at him, unruffled. 'I'm just finishing the SOFREM file, then I'm going home.'

'Finish it tomorrow,' Maltard cut him off. 'Close of play. Department's all cleared off home. You do the same.'

Without a word, Daniel put the top back on his Parker pen, engraved with his initials, a present from Véronique on their fifth wedding anniversary. He got to his feet, switched off his computer and his Minitel terminal, and put on his felt Homburg. Wearing a hat gives you a feeling of authority over someone who isn't, he thought to himself.

Sure enough, Jean Maltard suddenly looked a great deal smaller. He seemed to be shrinking before Daniel's very eyes. A bug shrinking down into the pile of the carpet, buzzing furiously. Daniel had only to tread it underfoot ...

'You're not going to get away with this!' said Maltard suddenly. 'You're waiting for a call from Desmoine, aren't you?' he added, with a venomous smile.

'He's already called actually.'

That was a shock to Maltard, who stared at Daniel dumbfounded. 'He's already called you?' He pronounced each word slowly and carefully.

'Yes,' replied Daniel evenly, putting on his coat.

'What did he want?' demanded Maltard.

'Breakfast. On Friday.'

'Breakfast with you,' said Maltard under his breath, as if muttering a spell that must not be spoken aloud for fear of the consequences.

'Yes, that's what he said.' Daniel bent down to slip a folder into his briefcase. There was a long silence, then he shut the clasps, the metallic snap signalling that it was time to leave.

The two men rode down in the lift without speaking, and parted in front of the entrance without shaking hands. Maltard watched as Daniel walked away, then went into the nearest café and ordered a double rum. The departing figure of his deputy in his coat and black hat haunted him for a good part of the night.

The secretary brought croissants and eggs which looked as if they were wearing woolly winter hats. Daniel supposed the crocheted accessories were there to keep the eggs at the right temperature. I'll have to tell Véronique, he thought. Jean-Bernard Desmoine sat opposite him. Both men were installed in large white leather armchairs near a window on the eighteenth floor of the SOGETEC building, overlooking Paris. Having such an elevated office must surely give its occupant a feeling of superiority.

'Tuck in,' said Desmoine, snatching the knitted hat off his egg. 'I'm very particular about how my eggs are cooked,' he added, smiling.

So that was it, thought Daniel, remembering at the same time that the correct way to break the top of a soft-boiled egg was with the back of a spoon, not a knife, as he did at home. He lifted the hat from his egg and rapped the top of the shell.

'Daniel, I won't beat about the bush. I was very

impressed by your analysis of the plans for the finance department.'

Daniel embarked on a suitably humble reply, but was interrupted before he could finish.

'No need to say anything,' said Desmoine. 'No false modesty, please. I'm not one for false compliments. Coffee?'

The director poured him a cup. If someone had told Daniel, just a few days before, that Desmoine himself would be serving him coffee, he, Daniel, the man who stood in line at the seventh-floor coffee machine, waiting for his plastic cup to drop …

Desmoine dipped the tip of a croissant in his coffee and chewed, at the same time proceeding to outline Daniel's future with wondrous precision and clarity: 'You see, I know a thing or two about people,' he announced with the confidence of those who have their own offices on the upper floors of tall buildings. 'People and business,' he mused. 'You don't get many surprises in our line of work. People are judged on their first year in the post; after that, they either develop or they don't. But no surprises. Do you get my drift?'

Daniel nodded, his mouth full of croissant, indicating that he did indeed get Desmoine's drift.

Desmoine took it upon himself to pour Daniel another cup of coffee. 'Important to drink coffee,' he added. 'Balzac drank litres of the stuff. You've read Balzac, of course.'

'Of course,' Daniel confirmed, never having read Balzac in his life.

'You really are a resourceful fellow. Why hasn't

SOGETEC got you in a more important post? You should have a position better suited to a man of your quality.'

'A position ...' muttered Daniel. 'You mean ...'

'Maltard's a complete arse,' interrupted Desmoine. 'Anyone can see that. But for reasons that are no concern of yours and which give me very little pleasure, I can assure you, I am obliged to keep him where he is. On the other hand, I want to promote you to director.'

Daniel stared at him, his croissant suspended over his cup.

'Daniel, I'm offering to make you director of one of SOGETEC's regional finance departments. I know you're based in Paris, but it's all I can offer you. Pierre Marcoussi heads the Rouen department, but he's leaving for health reasons. It's not official for the moment. You'll start in January.'

The hat. It was the hat that was responsible for the events that had turned Daniel's existence on its head in the last few days. He was convinced of that. Since he had taken to wearing it, the hat had conferred on him a kind of immunity to the torments of everyday life just by being there. Better still, it sharpened his mind and spurred him to take vitally important decisions. Without it, he would never have dared speak to Maltard as he had at the meeting. He would never have found himself on the eighteenth floor sharing a breakfast of soft-boiled eggs with Desmoine. In a strange way, he felt that something of the President was there in the hat. Something intangible. Some microscopic particle perhaps. But whatever it was, it had the power of destiny.

'Thank you,' Daniel muttered, addressing the hat as much as his superior.

'So you accept?' asked Desmoine, swallowing his last mouthful of croissant.

'I accept,' said Daniel, looking him straight in the eye.

'We'll be seeing each other again then,' said Desmoine, holding out his hand before bending over a third, hatless egg. 'This one's for me.' He smiled. Desmoine tapped the top with the handle of his teaspoon, making a small hole, then did the same at the other end, and threw his head back to swallow it down in one.

'Every morning. A raw egg. My little treat,' said Jean-Bernard Desmoine apologetically.

Less than a month later, Daniel, Véronique and Jérôme were back on the platform at Gare Saint-Lazare, this time waiting for train 06781 bound for Le Havre, first stop Rouen. Their five suitcases bulged; the furniture had been despatched in a removal van. Daniel, his black hat firmly on his head, gazed down the track, looking out for the train that would take them to their new life in a new place. Véronique squeezed his arm, and Jérôme sulked because he wouldn't be seeing his friends from school again.

Throughout the journey, Daniel thought back over his Paris years on the third floor of the SOGETEC building. His colleagues had clubbed together to buy him a leaving gift: a year's subscription to Canal +. For the past two years, the new pay TV channel had revolutionised office conversation. In the accounts department, Daniel couldn't fail to notice the sudden irruption of 'Canal' into the collective consciousness. Canal was '*un must*' as Florence, the communications manager, would say. Bernard Falgou and Michèle Carnavan swore by programmes that Daniel could only see as a hissing blur. The talk at the coffee machine was of feature films that had been in cinemas barely a year ago and were already on Canal. People who 'had Canal' could talk about them. The others could only listen in silence.

'Didn't you see it?' the sect of set-top box subscribers would exclaim.

'I haven't got Canal +.' The reply sounded like an admission of impotence, a fate to be endured.

Now, Daniel would have Canal +. He had received the channel's welcome letter to new subscribers, with its letterhead emblazoned with the slogan *'Canal +, c'est plus.'* All he had to do was visit one of their official distributors in Rouen, show them the letter and his subscriber number, and he would be presented with the hallowed decoder. From now on, at the coffee machine, Daniel would be able to talk to his new colleagues about last night's programmes, or the 8.30 film. He might even allow himself the wicked pleasure of asking some of them, 'You haven't got Canal? Oh, you really should …'

From what he had been told, the new apartment had one room more than their old one in the fifteenth *arrondissement*, their home for the past twelve years. The landlord had protested at their sudden departure, as had Jérôme's headmistress. Each time, Daniel had used the phrase: 'I'm so sorry, but in life there are some circumstances …' He took care to leave his words hanging, pregnant with meaning, a black hole absorbing any and all objections. What can you say to a man compelled by such mysterious, irresistible forces? Nothing, of course.

*

When they reached Rouen, the capital of Normandy, Daniel told the taxi driver their new address in the centre of town. After barely quarter of an hour in the car Véronique turned to him with that little frown that her husband was so fond of.

'Where's your hat?' she asked.

Time stood still for Daniel.

A long, icy shiver ran down his spine, as if someone had just walked on his grave. With horrible clarity, he pictured the hat on the luggage rack on the train. Not the rack where they had put their suitcases, but the one opposite. The hat was on the rack. His hat. Mitterrand's hat. In his haste to get off the train, Daniel, still unaccustomed to wearing a hat, had left it behind. He had just made the same mistake as the President of the Republic.

'We'll have to turn round,' he said in shock. 'Turn round immediately!' he yelled, from the back seat of the taxi.

The Peugeot 305 did an about-turn and accelerated back towards the station. Daniel leapt from the car and ran. But it was no good. The train had left. No one had taken the hat to the lost property office.

Days, weeks, months went by. Daniel called the central SNCF lost property office. When he realised he knew the number by heart, he knew, too, that he would never see Mitterrand's hat again.

That very evening, Fanny Marquant boarded the train at Le Havre heading for Paris Saint-Lazare. She put her suitcase on the rack above seat 88.

Directly opposite her in seat 86 was a young man with long hair, wearing mirrored sunglasses and a Walkman. The badges all over his leather jacket showed rockers with spiky bleached hair, also in black leather. Through his orange foam-covered headphones, Fanny could make out the 'The Final Countdown', Europe's hit single. Fanny personally preferred listening to a new singer on the block, a redhead with anxious eyes by the name of Mylène Farmer whose kooky style and romantic lyrics appealed to her far more than the electric guitar solos of some bleach-blond rockers. You could tell Mylène Farmer was well read; she knew her Edgar Allan Poe and Baudelaire, which Fanny, herself a keen reader and writer, approved of.

Fanny took out a pink Clairefontaine notebook where she had written the first three pages of a story called, simply, 'Édouard'. The Prix Balbec short story competition was offering a prize of 3,000 francs and publication in the local supplement of *Ouest-France*. The prize was to be awarded in March at the Grand Hôtel de Cabourg. Fanny had been writing for as long as she could remember, first diaries in little locked notebooks, and later pieces of creative writing she kept to herself until she finally plucked up the courage to send one in to a competition. 'The Bouquet' was the winning entry; there was no prize money, but she had never before felt such a sense of recognition and pride. 'Change of Address' came third in another local contest and 'An Afternoon at the Harbour' was read out at Le Havre Theatre Festival.

The theme of this year's Prix Balbec was 'A True Story' and Fanny was attempting to record for posterity how Édouard had come into her life.

Fanny, a secretary at the tax office in Le Havre, had been having an affair with Édouard Lanier for two years, five months and two weeks now. Édouard Lanier worked in Paris as an executive at Chambourcy, the famous yogurt brand splashed over billboards and TV screens everywhere. Édouard was also married with children.

Early on in their relationship, he had been careless enough to tell Fanny: 'I love you. I'm going to leave my wife ...' A moment of madness in the first flush of romance when he was still young enough to believe life would turn out just as he wanted. Realising the dizzying implications of his words, he had been saying ever since that he just needed time. It was his eternal refrain: 'I need time ... you need to give me time ... all I need is time.' He went through every possible variation. Over the last two years, Édouard had become more obsessed with time than the most meticulous Swiss watchmaker. He needed time to speak to his wife, time to make her understand and accept him starting over with someone else – and it was turning their sweet love affair sour.

These days, in the hotel room in the Batignolles district of Paris where they met once, sometimes twice, a month, when the fun and games were over, Édouard would tie his tie in the light from the closed shutters, looking wary and waiting for Fanny to ask timidly: 'Have you spoken to your wife yet?' His face would fall and he would emit a barely audible sigh. 'You know how it is, I just need time,' he would mutter, shaking his head.

And still Fanny went on loving Édouard. She had loved him from the moment he put down his briefcase in the compartment of the Le Havre–Paris train. Tall and slim with salt and pepper hair and a dimple on his chin, he ticked all Fanny's boxes in the looks department. The wedding ring on his left hand had not escaped her attention, but she was even more struck when it was slipped off shortly afterwards. It left behind an imprint, a little circle running around his third finger which faded over the course of the journey from Normandy to the capital.

All it had taken was a magazine falling to the floor, Édouard bending down to pick it up and handing it back to her with a smile, to seal the start of a passionate affair. If Fanny closed her eyes, she could go back to that one moment which had changed the course of her life. It was like an advert for cologne: man gets on train, pretty woman sits in carriage reading magazine, train starts moving, woman drops magazine, man bends down to pick it up, meaningful looks are exchanged, manly odours mingled with the scent of cologne waft towards her, woman swoons. Life had handed her one of those cheesy moments usually seen only on TV screens and girl-meets-boy American romantic comedies.

Since then, Fanny had come to know the Le Havre–Paris route by heart, along with the occasional detour for a brief encounter in Rouen or Trouville. An average of forty-five trips a year, always paid for by Édouard and always taking place outside the Easter, summer and Christmas holidays which, it goes without saying, he spent far away from her, with his family. At the age of twenty-seven, Fanny had achieved the status of mistress. The question of whether she might one day be promoted to official wife was still up in the air, as was the possibility of promotion to executive secretary at the tax office. Her application for that position was 'under careful consideration'. The recruitment process for her life role was at the same stage, 'under careful consideration' by Édouard, whose inertia was thus on a par with that of the civil service.

'You're perfectly happy with the situation. You'll never leave your wife, I know you won't,' she'd once said angrily.

'That's not true,' he had objected. 'I love you and I'm not going to spend the rest of my life with my wife, I just can't do it. We've stopped making love. There's nothing between us any more.'

'Well, leave her then!'

Édouard had shaken his head, looking stricken, and uttered his favourite phrase: 'You need to give me time.'

Fanny had fallen back onto the pillows and stared up at the ceiling of the hotel room. This is going nowhere, it occurred to her, looking at him – and not for the first time. The history we share is a chance meeting on a train, our life together now is confined to a hotel room, and we have no future.

Fanny was right. It was difficult to go anywhere but the bedroom with Édouard. There was no way they could walk down the street holding hands or go round the shops together. The one time they spent a whole weekend in Trouville, Édouard had convinced himself that everyone he knew was going to appear as if by chance at any moment. A work colleague, a friend of his, or worse, a friend of his wife's might be having a day out in the Norman fishing village. What if someone saw them? It was the same with restaurants. They had never ventured beyond the confines of Batignolles, where Édouard knew no one. But even there, the idea that some acquaintance might decide to dine at the same place made him turn round every time the door opened.

When they were together in Paris, Édouard would tell his wife he was on a business trip to another part of the country or abroad. This meant swotting up on train timetables, airport strikes and any local festivals he might be expected to know about, having supposedly been in town for them. Fanny understood that the pressure to stay on his toes was a burden on him; she, on the other hand, answered to no one. There was no one waiting up for her but her Minitel screen, on which she and Édouard planned dates and sometimes exchanged messages during the night. It was as if the machine had been invented with illicit lovers in mind.

It was impossible to call Édouard at home and difficult to get hold of him at the office, so they met by dialling 3615 Aline. Their aliases popped up a few times a month among the names listed in flickering columns on the left of the Minitel's black screen. Édouard was 'Alpha75' and Fanny 'Sweetiepie'.

Whenever Édouard found a gap in his diary, he would leave a message for Sweetiepie. *Free 22nd–23rd, how about you?* to which Sweetiepie would reply, *I'll be there, same time, same place.* Less often, they would meet virtually during the night. Édouard would creep out of the marital bed (taking great care to avoid creaky floorboards), turn on the screen, wait for the dial-up tone and meet Sweetiepie at the agreed time. They would exchange sweet nothings and promises. 'You have a message,' it would flash at the top of the screen.

Sometimes, Sweetiepie found her correspondent wasn't Alpha75 after all but someone making obscene proposals she chose not to take up. As for Alpha75, he was occasionally contacted by men asking if he was free that night and up for real-life action or just a chat. Romance found a way through the murky new world of electronic connections.

Fanny had been sucked into a bittersweet 'relationship' which revolved around seeing her loved one for a quickie a few times a month. She wished she could find the courage to end it with Édouard the next time she saw him, but she knew she didn't have it in her. This was not the first time she had felt so unsure, both of the situation and herself. If nothing changed between them, it could carry on like this for years.

She could find nothing to write in her pink notebook, so Fanny put the lid back on her pen and dozed off. Two hours later, she opened her eyes. She would soon be in Paris and the rain was lashing against the window. She sighed, remembering she had not brought an umbrella, when her gaze fell on a black hat on the luggage rack. She looked around. There were only five passengers left on this late train, all of them sitting a good distance away from her. The felt hat could not belong to any of them. Fanny stood up as the train braked, took down the hat and put it on. She looked at her reflection in the darkened window. The hat suited her, and it would be just the thing to keep the rain off her hair.

The black felt brim acted like a visor, compressing the space around her and marking out a distinct horizon. In Batignolles, a man did a double take as he passed her. What kind of image was she projecting, walking along in the moonlight in her denim mini-skirt, high heels, silver jacket and black hat? That of a hip eighties girl, young, free and sexy, perhaps a little bit forward ... She stopped to look at herself in a mirror in the window of a boutique.

The hat gave her jaw line a new air of distinction; she had put her hair up in a bun to help keep it in place. Perhaps she should always wear it up like this and put on a man's black felt hat every time she went out. Donning the new accessory had made her feel somehow powerful; it had the same effect as the designer clothes she so rarely treated herself to. Take her Saint Laurent skirt and Rykiel heels, for example. All she had to do was put on the YSL skirt and she immediately felt more attractive. The same went for the shoes, which had cost her almost a quarter of a month's salary: as soon as she slipped them on and did up the little straps, she felt taller, straighter and more significant. She walked completely differently, strutting along with confidence, and only she knew it was down to the hidden powers of the Rykiel shoes.

The rain had stopped and Fanny took off the hat. She noticed two letters embossed in gold on the leather band running round the inside of the hat: F.M. Could fate really have meant the hat for her? Here were Fanny Marquant's own initials.

'Well, then ... I'm not letting go of you, my friend, no way', she murmured, stroking the hat.

Then she tied her hair up, put the hat back on and set off down the road with an even more determined stride.

The Batignolles district was deserted but for a few indistinct figures far off in the distance, disappearing into the shadows of apartment blocks. The hotel was not far from here and Édouard would be waiting for her in their room. He would be watching TV or else lying on the bed reading *Le Monde*.

As she walked through the lobby, she passed the receptionist. He nodded at her with a knowing smile. Fanny could not stand the man, who knew all the ins and outs of her love life. With his leering smile and creepy nod, she could imagine him roaming the corridors after dark, listening out for the sighs of lovers forced to meet at this crappy hotel. She began climbing the stairs, dragging her case after her, convinced he was looking at her legs. Second floor, room 26.

As she reached the door, she could hear the television

was on. A fierce debate was raging, a chorus of voices speaking all at once. It could only be *Droit de réponse*, the talk show Édouard liked to watch. The guests sat around the set smoking, shouting and getting worked up; as things got more and more heated, the host, Michel Polac, simply looked on in amusement, puffing on his pipe and narrowing his eyes. Fanny knocked on the door just as the round-up of the week in pictures was starting: Siné, Plantu, Wolinski and Cabu had drawn cartoons to illustrate the news. The actress Monique Tarbès provided the ironic commentary, rounding off with a jaunty 'See you next week!' worthy of a market trader.

'Come in, it's open.' Édouard was lying on the bed in his open shirt and boxers, and as Fanny came in he propped a pillow behind his back and stared at her. 'What's with the hat?'

'Nice to see you too,' she replied, bending down to give him a kiss.

Édouard kissed her tenderly, stroking up and down her neck the way she liked to be touched. He was about to move up to her hair and brush the hat off, when she stepped back sharply.

'Hands off my hat.'

'*Your* hat?' he said, emphasising the possessive with a note of sarcasm. 'Where did you get it from anyway?'

'It's a secret, but it is my hat.'

On the television screen, a man with a cigar hanging from his mouth was busily stating the obvious. In protest, a small, bald man leapt out of his chair and appealed to Michel Polac, who once again appeared delighted to sit back and watch his programme sliding into chaos.

'It's a man's hat,' Édouard pointed out. He got up to turn the volume down.

'So?' said Fanny, readjusting it over her hair.

'So that means a man gave it to you,' continued Édouard, staring straight at her.

Fanny gave him a strange little smile. 'Are you jealous?'

'I might be. You come into our room wearing a present from someone else …'

The mood in the room had suddenly shifted. Fanny studied Édouard carefully. She loved his body, his hands; she loved his face, his voice, his hair. For the last two and a half years, she had loved all of that. She had been jealous of a phantom wife she had never laid eyes on and whose existence meant she could not be with Édouard. He, on the other hand, had never been jealous, yet this evening she could see the signs of it appearing on his face. How far could she take this little game with the hat Édouard took to be a gift from another man?

All the way, she realised in a burst of lucidity, surprising even herself. In the space of a few moments, the felt hat had emerged as the source of strength she had waited so long for. All at once, the cowardice which had prevented her talking to Édouard, perhaps even breaking it off, had vanished. Now she understood Michel Polac's approach: push it as far as it will go until the whole thing explodes, then sit back and survey the damage. Fanny shivered with fear and excitement. She took a step back, perched on the table and tilted her head to one side, all the while keeping her eyes on Édouard. She was about to leap into the unknown and it was a delicious feeling, more satisfying than any sexual position.

'Yes, the hat was a present,' she said softly.

'Who gave it to you?'

The question opened a gaping hole at Fanny's feet. 'A man,' she heard herself reply. 'A man I met on the train.'

'Like me?' Édouard instinctively pulled the white sheet up over his chest, as if literally to protect his feelings.

'Yes, like you.'

'How old is he? It's an old man's hat!' cried Édouard, too loudly for the time of night (though no sound came from behind the walls of sleeping Batignolles).

'He's older than you, it's true,' began Fanny, gazing off into space, 'but it doesn't matter. He's not handsome the way you are; he's beautiful in a different way. He's thoughtful and considerate, he loves me and he wants to live with me. I borrowed his hat – it's a little game we play – and I wore it all round Le Havre. I even wore it once when we were making love – I put it on and got on top ...'

Édouard stared at her, rooted to the spot.

'So he bought me one of my own, just like his. He got my initials put in it and gave it to me to remind me of him.'

Fanny took off her hat and smoothly passed it to Édouard, who turned it over to read the gold letters inside.

'You'll never leave your wife and I'll never be anything more than the girl you meet in hotels at weekends, so I'm going to leave you, Édouard. Like that Gainsbourg song:

"Je suis venu te dire que je m'en vais."

The words had come out of her mouth perfectly calmly and yet, inside, Fanny was in turmoil.

Édouard breathed deeply, keeping his eyes on her, trying to decide how to react – though since Fanny appeared to have made up her mind, his options were somewhat limited. He had lost. He had lost her.

'Fine,' he said crossly. 'You could have saved me a wasted weekend coming here. You could have just told me by Minitel.'

He got off the bed and grabbed his trousers. Fanny watched as though from a distance, as if Édouard were no more than a silhouette moving in the sunlight at the far end of a beach. He put on his trousers and angrily buttoned his shirt, his fingers fumbling with the tiny mother-of-pearl buttons.

'Waiting until half past midnight to tell me that ...' he grumbled, scowling at her. 'You want to leave me but I'm the one who's getting out of here!' he announced before kneeling down to look for his loafers under the bed.

It was as if the floor was on fire, as though the whole room was about to go up in flames. Yet in spite of his fury, he was surprised to find himself feeling a sense of relief. All the questions about his wife would finally come to an end now, along with his terse replies about needing time. He was tired of trotting out the same old empty excuses. OK, he had been dumped, but the truth was the break-up took a weight off him. As he put on his jacket, he was ashamed to admit he was both mortified and glad. Perhaps that was the most painful part of it.

'Aren't you even going to try and stop me?'

'No,' replied Édouard breathlessly. 'No. You're cheating on me, you're leaving me, I'm going.' He did up the metal strap of his Kelton quartz watch and stood in front of Fanny. 'Goodbye,' he said coldly, 'you can keep the room until midday tomorrow.' Then he picked up his overnight bag.

'Where are you going?' she asked gently, though the answer mattered little to her.

'Maybe Lyon. That's where everyone thinks I am,' he replied, opening the door and slamming it behind him.

Fanny leant against the table, listening to Édouard's footsteps fading along the corridor, and closed her eyes. Her head was spinning. She slowly took off her jacket, then her skirt, her bra and shoes and finally her knickers and looked at herself in the bathroom mirror, naked save for the hat on her head.

She took her perfume, Solstice, out of her bag and sprayed it over the pillows to mask the smell of Édouard. She took off the hat, laid it on the bed and turned out the light. She slid under the sheets and closed her eyes. Sitting beside her on top of the bed covers, the hat was caught in the moonlight. Fanny brushed her fingers over the soft felt before falling asleep.

The winter sun shone through the net curtains, casting pools of light on Fanny's breasts. She slowly opened her eyes. The events of the previous night came back to her bit by bit, unlike dreams which drift away the moment you wake up: Édouard under the sheets, listening to her; Édouard scrambling to his feet; Édouard inspecting the initials inside the hat, then the sound of the door slamming shut and, 'You could have saved me a wasted weekend.' Then his footsteps in the corridor.

So it was over. It wasn't a dream, it really was over. Never again would Fanny return to the hotel room in Batignolles; never again would they fix secret dates in Paris or at Norman ports; never again would she turn on the Minitel in the middle of the night looking for Alpha75. It was over. How could you disappear from someone's life just like that? Perhaps, when all was said and done, it was just as easy to leave someone's life as to enter it. A stroke of fate and a few words could be enough to start a relationship. A stroke of fate and a few words could end it too. Before it, nothingness. Afterwards, emptiness. What was left of Édouard? Zilch. Not even a poxy present to pin her feelings on. No cigarette lighter, no key-ring, no scarf, still less a photo of the two of them together or a letter with his handwriting on. Nothing.

She lay there for a long while, the patches of sunlight warming her breasts and belly, before turning her head to the left. Still sitting on the sheet, the hat had not moved an inch. She remembered that you weren't supposed to put hats on beds, a stupid old wives' tale like the ones about ladders and black cats. Fanny didn't believe in that sort of hocus pocus. All this fuss over a hat, she mused. So who was this F.M.? If only he knew what a chain of events his felt Homburg had set in motion ...

She tried to put a face to the man she had invented the previous evening, that wonderful lover who had given her a hat just like his own and had her initials put in it as a sign of his affection. No man she had ever known would do such a thing, would ever have such class, such panache. Was he tall, slender, or average build? Did he have brown, blond or grey hair?

No face came to mind. She had lied for the first time in as long as she could remember and it had worked. At no point had Édouard stood up and declared, 'I don't believe you! You're lying.' No. The idea that Fanny might be spinning a yarn had not even crossed his mind. For that matter, it occurred to her, he had never read a single one of her stories. She was reminded of the subject of the competition: 'A True Story'. The story of Fanny and Édouard had come to an end. And all because of a hat. That was the tale she must tell.

From the moment she had sat down at the table of the little café on Place Félix-Lobligeois, she had not put down her pen. She filled page after page of the pink notebook with her rounded handwriting, drawing little circles on top of every 'i'. The words told the story of her split from Édouard, the misunderstanding over the hat and all the feelings she was experiencing: relief, anxiety, sadness and nostalgia. Towards the end of her account, she wrote: 'This hat was no longer of use to me; it had served its purpose, and even though it bore my initials, I resolved to leave it somewhere in the city.'

Leave the hat behind? Fanny chewed the end of her pen. It struck her as a romantic idea. If she discarded the hat somewhere in Paris before getting her train, her story could reflect the truth right up to the end. This small act of sacrifice might even bring her luck. Filled with doubt, she looked up from her page to see a gypsy and her daughter walking towards her. Fanny smiled and turned away.

'I don't want anything,' she said.

'I'm a clairvoyant, I'll tell you your fortune,' said the woman, whose dark-brown hair was swept up under a red headscarf. She had a tattoo between her eyes and a line under her bottom lip.

'No, I'd rather you didn't,' Fanny insisted, smiling once again, 'really.' She looked down at the child, who was staring at her oddly.

'Yes, I'm going to tell you.'

Fanny shook her head and withdrew her hands.

The woman placed her dark, papery hand on the hat but pulled it away again immediately as though the felt were boiling hot. 'It's not yours, this hat.' Her expression had changed – she looked almost frightened. Her hand hovered above the hat. 'This is a man's hat, he is very powerful,' she said, crossing herself.

'Oi, you! Stop bothering the customers!' shouted a waiter with a grey goatee.

'No, it's all right,' Fanny told him.

'It's not all right, young lady. This is my terrace and I'm not putting up with that.'

'Whose hat is it?' Fanny asked regardless.

'You know him, everyone they know him.'

'No,' replied Fanny, 'you're wrong, I don't know him.'

'Yes, you do.'

'Well then, tell me his name.'

'You give me money, give me twenty francs.'

'No, I don't have twenty francs for that.'

'Give me fifteen.'

'No, I'm sorry.'

'Will you leave the young lady alone!'

The gypsies stepped away as the waiter came over, flicking his tea towel as though trying to scare off cats.

'They'll tell you any old rubbish and then you look down and find your wallet's gone. They pulled the same trick last week,' he grumbled.

Fanny watched the woman and her little girl disappear around the corner. *You know him.* It was ridiculous, how could you know the owner of a hat you'd found on a train? She must not let herself be put off. She had to finish her story; she had poured two and a half years of her life into it. If she could land the Prix Balbec, it would be the best possible consolation prize for an unhappy love affair.

An hour and a quarter later, Fanny was beginning to doubt anything interesting ever happened in parks. Her feet had taken her far beyond Batignolles to the gates of Parc Monceau on Boulevard de Courcelles. She had gone in, passing the usual park wildlife of children and old people. As she stood on the main path looking at the row of benches, it occurred to her to place the hat on one of them. The fourth one along was empty; she put it down there and retreated to watch discreetly from the bench opposite. No one had seen her do it; now all she had to do was wait.

But since then, nobody had stopped or even turned to look at the solitary black hat. She wasn't so sure now about her poetic gesture; after all the hat belonged to her, it even had her initials inside it, and what did it matter really if the ending of her story was true or not?

Just as she was getting up to retrieve it, a bearded man in jeans and a sheepskin jacket stopped beside the bench. He seemed to hesitate for a moment before sitting down. He was wearing round, black-rimmed glasses and must have been about sixty. He turned to look at the hat, observing it as though it was a silent, mysterious creature. He reached for it and turned it over. Then, bizarrely, he held it up to his nose and seemed to sniff it. He smiled and glanced at his watch, then he stood up, turned back to face the hat, paused, and snatched it up again. Fanny watched him leave. He held the headwear in his hand, without putting it on. He disappeared out of the entrance to the park.

Fanny took out her fountain pen and wrote: 'The man with the grey beard took the hat away. Who was he? I will never know.' She suddenly felt incredibly tired. Perhaps it was only just sinking in that she had really left Édouard. After a brief dizzy spell she could not bring herself to record in her story, Fanny stood up and went the same way as the man who had taken the hat.

She passed through the wrought-iron gates and stopped on the pavement. 'He is very powerful,' the gypsy had said, crossing herself. 'You know him, everyone they know him.' Fanny could not take her eyes off the cover of *Le Nouvel Observateur*, which had been blown up and plastered all over the newspaper kiosk. The picture showed François Mitterrand with a red scarf around his neck, a dark coat and a black felt hat on his head. He was staring into the camera with a mischievous glint in his eye, and Fanny had the distinct impression the President was looking straight at her.

Sicilian lemon, bergamot, green mandarin, tangerine, cypress, basil, juniper berry, cumin, sandalwood, white musk, ylang-ylang, patchouli, amber and vanilla. Pierre Aslan identified the scent as Eau d'Hadrien, created by Annick Goutal in 1981. But there was also another perfume on the hat, a more recent addition: bergamot, pink jasmine, sweet myrrh, vanilla, iris and tonka bean. Pierre could have recited the ingredients of the second scent forwards or backwards. It was that mythical perfume Solstice. His perfume. Invented by him, Pierre Aslan, the nose.

He could not have said why he had picked up the hat. He had long since given up trying to find reasons for his bizarre behaviour, which had previously been a source of such confusion. He sniffed the hat again: there were definitely two perfumes, Eau d'Hadrien, for men, and Solstice, for women. The felt of the hat was impregnated with Eau d'Hadrien; Solstice was only just beginning to take its place.

Pierre Aslan, who hadn't created anything for eight years now, was not in Parc Monceau by chance. For the last five years he had been seeing a psychoanalyst, Dr Fremenberg, and had formed the habit of walking in the park for quarter of an hour or so each week before his appointments. Five years of spending six hundred francs a week for very little result. In less than ten minutes it would be time for another of these silent sessions to begin. Fremenberg practically never spoke. As a committed Freudian, he practised a form of free-floating attention, a listening technique that gave the patient the impression that his analyst was thinking about something else or was actually asleep.

Now it was ten minutes into the session. Pierre lay on the green velvet Napoleon III couch, staring as usual at the African fetish in the alcove to the left of the window. The dark wooden statue was of a man with an elongated face, like Munch's *Scream*, whose abnormally small body was enhanced by an erect penis. Reflected against the wall of the alcove by the spotlight, the statue appeared larger than it was.

Fremenberg liked primitive art, especially statuettes, fetishes and canes. His consulting room had a good dozen of these wooden objects, sculpted by tribes who followed scary magic rituals dating back to the beginning of time. These trophies were displayed on modern plinths with brushed steel or black Plexiglas legs. Pierre had always found them abhorrent, displayed as they were totally out of context.

It wasn't so much the works themselves as seeing

them exhibited in the bourgeois setting of a Haussmann-designed apartment that rendered them hostile. They seemed to be suffering, and as a result to be emanating curses. Éric, his son, who was only interested in the top 50 and his skateboard, would have said they were 'freaky'. And he would be right, thought Pierre, as Fremenberg cleared his throat briefly before lapsing back into silence.

In the beginning, when he had started coming to these inert sessions, Pierre had really made an effort to express his feelings. 'You're there to talk about yourself ...' his wife had said. 'So talk, tell him what's wrong.' And Pierre had talked. He'd talked about the fragrances that hadn't worked, the scents that had resisted definition, particularly the one he called 'angel's essence', in reference to the angel's share, those few drops of a vintage wine or brandy which evaporate through the cork, and even through the waxed cork covering. To Pierre, angel's essence was what you smelt when you sniffed a perfume, although it wasn't actually one of the ingredients. It wasn't listed anywhere. It existed without being there.

A sepulchral silence had greeted his confidences. Aslan was disappointed that for once his profession elicited no expression of interest. So he tried another tack. He talked about his marriage. He began by describing his wife, the famous pianist and Bach specialist Esther Kerwitcz, who travelled the world performing concert after concert and whose face often graced the pages of fashion magazines. Her beautiful green eyes could be seen in *Elle*, *Vogue*, *Le Figaro Madame*, *Vanity Fair* and even *Egoïste*, where Herb Ritts had immortalised her clasped hands as they rested on the keys. These revelations were also received in oppressive silence.

In the following sessions he had spoken about his early childhood and how he had first become interested in scents while in his grandfather's Provençal kitchen garden. Neither the peppery smell of a rubbed tomato leaf, nor the mellow, enveloping odour of mint elicited the slightest reaction from his analyst. Even when Pierre had talked about his son Éric and how he worried about what would become of him, Fremenberg still did not react.

In three and a half months, he had not heard his analyst speak. He was greeted at the start of each session by a discreet handshake and a silent nod. No words were uttered; there was never a hello or a good evening. At the end of the session, the handing over of the 500-franc note, with its 100-franc brother, caused Fremenberg to give a severe little frown, as though the acceptance of money was a painful ritual that had to be endured.

One day, Aslan turned up unwillingly for his session and pulled a face as he stretched out on the couch. 'I have to warn you that I slept very badly last night,' he began.

The silence of the consulting room was broken by a voice saying gravely, 'A bad dream perhaps?'

And it seemed to Pierre as though Fremenberg spoke in the tone of a waiter offering a dessert, with that mixture of deference and authority that expects the listener to respond promptly.

Pierre described the dream that had disturbed his sleep. Carnivorous plants had climbed out of his wife's piano and rampaged through the flat until they reached the perfume organ. Their spines and leaves had swept through the precious little bottles, knocking one of them to the floor where it smashed. But there was no odour. Pierre picked up the shards and sniffed them. Nothing. So he opened all the bottles and found they contained only water. The mutant plants began to bleed and shrivel on the floor, whereupon Pierre was seized by an irrational anguish. He had to save the plants or else the apartment would burst into flames. He had woken up just as the first flames had started licking at his study door.

As he finished describing his dream he turned to Fremenberg, who was taking notes with a Montblanc Meisterstück. His face looked completely serene, he was practically smiling. It had been a long time since Pierre had given anyone that much pleasure and it immediately made him feel more confident. 'You see, Fremenberg is peculiar – everyone says so – but he is an excellent therapist; he's going to help you. You seem happier; it seems to me you're getting better,' Esther had said. Yes, at that moment, Pierre was feeling better.

A few weeks later though, it was back to the long silent sessions. Pierre didn't have a dream he could describe and he sensed this was a disappointment to his analyst. That made him feel guilty. Lying on the couch, he could feel Fremenberg's disapproving presence behind him. The return to square one made him feel more despairing than ever.

A 'disappointment' was the worst possible thing to be and Pierre was now convinced that he was the walking embodiment of the word. He who had once been the brilliant star of French perfume and who from the age of nineteen to forty-four had risen relentlessly through the firmament! He had gone from lab assistant to 'nose' in less than three years, astounding his peers with his audacious combinations and encyclopedic knowledge of scents. He had been capable of recognising and categorising more than ten thousand scents and had even invented a new language, a veritable personal Esperanto, to describe them – *kérakac*, for the odour of wet, burnt wood, *varvine* for limestone heated by the sun, *pergaz* for seaweed abandoned on the shore at dusk …

He had created seven perfumes before his imagination had withered and he had become a disappointment. A disappointment to his backers, who no longer recognised in him the genius creator of Solstice, Alba or Sheraz. A disappointment to his wife, who found herself married to a husk of a man who hung aimlessly about the flat dragging himself from bedroom to sitting room. But crucially and above all he had become a disappointment to himself. The brands that had previously paid him a fortune to sniff little strips of paper diagnosed a creative block that would soon pass. It hadn't. After eight years during which he had created nothing, no one mentioned that possibility any more. Pierre Aslan had been great, now he wasn't.

From time to time in order to keep on the right side of his analyst, Pierre would invent a dream. Despite not remembering any of his dreams from the night before his session, he would nevertheless serve up a good yarn to entertain Fremenberg. The last time he'd done it, the dream had involved a purple bat that had flown into the cellar and bumped into some hessian sacks filled with rotting rose petals. Fremenberg had liked that. Occasionally, Pierre would have a quick fantasy of punching his analyst or striking him with one of those obscene fetishes.

This session, nothing came to mind as he stretched out on the couch. He rested the hat on his thighs and stroked it gently to pass the time. The repetitive movement of his fingers against the felt evoked an image from his childhood

– Aladdin rubbing his brass lamp to summon up the genie to fulfil his every wish. That thought linked to a hat found in the park might interest Fremenberg. Nevertheless Pierre decided not to share it with him.

As Pierre walked home, he passed the bench and hesitated. Should he put the hat back on it? Its owner might come back hoping to find it there. A young woman pushing a pram stopped, checked that the baby inside was sleeping soundly, then sat down and opened *Télé-Poche* which had a kitsch picture of Joan Collins on the front. Now it would be difficult to go over to the bench, put the hat down and leave in silence without appearing like a lunatic or a mad fetishist. And he didn't feel able to explain to the girl – who was undoubtedly an au pair, and probably foreign – that he'd found the hat an hour earlier on the bench.

No, it was much better just to keep the hat, at least for now. Pierre looked inside the hat again and this time the two gold letters made him think of FM radio – another curious association that might have been of interest to Fremenberg – then he put the hat on and slowly smoothed the black brim between his thumb and forefinger. It had been a long time since his fingers had made that particular gesture, which drew an imaginary line in front of his eyes.

As Aslan moved off he thought back to his very first hat, a grey felt hat with a narrow brim, bought in Harrods in 1967. His purchase of that piece of headgear had been the occasion of a lively encounter with Tony Curtis.

The actor had just put the hat down amongst the others when Aslan had picked it up to try it on. Tony Curtis had remonstrated, saying that he intended to buy it, but Aslan had stood his ground: the hat had been on the table; if the actor had wanted to buy it, he should have kept it in his hand. The head of department had watched this exchange in anguished silence, then apologised profusely to the star, not knowing how to put things right – there wasn't a single other hat like that in the whole store.

The run-in had turned good-natured when Curtis and Aslan had tried the hat on in front of the mirror one after the other to see who it suited best.

'You, definitely,' the actor had declared, magnanimously holding the hat out to Aslan, who, not wanting to be beholden, had hurried over to the perfume counter to buy the cologne he'd detected Curtis wearing and offered it to him.

'As the saying goes in French: *nous sommes quittes?*' he'd said, raising his hat in farewell.

Many years later, he'd come across the actor at a reception in Los Angeles. 'You've forgotten your hat, Mister Nose,' a voice had said behind him and they had reminisced pleasurably about their encounter at Harrods. That was the era when Aslan still socialised, and there were photographs to prove it. He'd been wearing a dinner jacket with a rose buttonhole and Esther was in a long dress. What remained of that style and elegance? Nothing. He had grown a beard six years ago, trimming it every three months, and instead of impeccable charcoal-grey suits, he wore an old threadbare sheepskin jacket, which would not have looked out of place on the park's gardeners. At the very lowest point of his depression, he had decided to sort out his clothes. It had been dramatic. He had taken all his suits, overcoats, jackets and hats to the Salvation Army. Some had been worn out but others were perfectly wearable. The only item Pierre would have liked to hold on to would have been 'Tony Curtis's hat', but he'd left it on an aeroplane a few years earlier.

Perhaps it doesn't go with your beard. At three in the morning he grabbed his glasses from the bedside table and got up without waking Esther. On his return from the session with his analyst, Esther had been playing the first movement of Bach's Toccata in C minor, practising one particular passage. Pierre had followed the sound of the Steinway until he reached the sitting room where he found her concentrating on the keys, her back to the door, her hair up in a bun. She repeated four or five notes several times. Each time they sounded the same, but to her they obviously weren't right. It was a question of touch or duration. The timing was probably only out by a nano-second, but she wasn't satisfied.

Demand for absolute perfection characterised both their professions. A tiny detail became a huge obstacle and they could only rest easy once they had surmounted it. The repetition of notes might last a few minutes or it might go on all afternoon. A perfume could be created after a few weeks, or several months and sometimes several years of research. The composition of Shalimar had been a fluke. In a trial, Jacques Guerlain had poured a few drops of synthetic vanilla into a bottle of Jicky, and he had created Shalimar. Patou's 1000 on the other hand had taken years and years of research and no less than a thousand trials, hence its name. Esther was perfectly capable of practising the same phrase a thousand times if necessary. He had intended to withdraw without disturbing her work, but a floorboard had creaked under his foot. Esther turned round.

'You frightened me! What's that hat?'

'It's a black hat,' Pierre had replied

'I see that, but where did you get it?'

'In a little second-hand designer shop on Boulevard de Courcelles.'

'I thought they only sold women's clothes.'

'So did I, but it was in the window; it had just been dropped off.' Pierre was thinking on his feet. His wife was already finding it hard to take the old sheepskin jacket and the threadbare Girbaud jeans. She certainly wouldn't approve of him wearing a hat found on a bench. The boutique, *Des marques et vous*, was on his way to Fremenberg's, so it was perfectly believable that he might have spotted the hat in the window and gone in to try it on.

'It's been a long time since you last wore a hat,' said Esther, looking at him closely. 'It does suit you, but …' she was frowning, her head on one side, 'perhaps it doesn't go with your beard; it makes you look …'

'What does it make me look?'

'A bit strange.'

Pierre had walked over to the mirror above the mantelpiece and didn't think he looked strange. Esther had repeated the notes from Bach then asked him how the session with Fremenberg had gone. 'Well,' said Pierre without elaborating. At that moment he felt as if he could spend the rest of his life leaning on the mantelpiece, the hat on his head, contemplating his wife's reflection as she played Bach. The repetition of the notes helped create a reassuring impression of eternity.

Perhaps it doesn't go with your beard. The moonlight was filtering through the net curtains into the sitting room. Pierre nearly knocked into the coffee table but soon oriented himself by the dark mass of the sofa. Once out of the door, he crossed the corridor, passed his son's bedroom and reached the bathroom, locking himself in.

The fluorescent light blinked as it warmed up. He closed his eyes painfully then flicked the switch off. Candles. There were candles in the broom cupboard. Blinded by the harsh light which was still imprinted on his retina, he went out of the bathroom and felt his way to the cupboard. The candles were stored in a cardboard box along with a Bic lighter in case of a power cut.

There, that's much better, he thought, lighting the first candle which he put on the side of the basin. He lit another, then a third. He opened a drawer, took out a small pair of golden scissors, leant towards the mirror and took hold of his cheek between thumb and forefinger. Grey and black hairs fell in a fine rain into the basin.

A good twenty minutes later, he had no more than five days' worth of beard. He ran the tap and bathed his face in hot water. He wetted his shaving brush under the scalding stream of water and began to rub the shaving soap in little circular movements. The white foam thickened into a cream which he spread in wide bands across his cheeks, chin, mouth and neck, before freeing his lips with a wipe of his thumb.

He put the razor just under his ear, held his breath and drew the blade down to the bottom of his neck. His skin was revealed, soft and smooth. The foam, dotted with black and grey, whirled down the plughole. Pierre wiped the steamed-up mirror, attacked his left cheek, his right cheek, his neck, moustache and chin, puffing out his lower lip for the finishing touches. All that was left now on his face was a few traces of white soap.

He grabbed a towel, put it under the hot tap, and buried his face in its softness. He stayed like that for a good minute with his eyes closed, then slowly lowered the towel to look in the mirror. It was like bumping into an old friend he hadn't seen for a long time. The mirror reflected back a well-known face, a man who looked like Pierre Aslan.

The sun was shining into the consulting room, making the sheen on the old masks glow against the white wall.

'I shaved my beard off,' said Pierre. 'I shaved my beard off and I have a hat,' he added.

As usual his declaration was met with silence.

'If I hadn't put in a drop of sweet myrrh, Solstice would

have been different. If I hadn't found the hat, I wouldn't have shaved,' he said more loudly.

He found his reasoning very compelling. It was as simple and brilliant as a mathematical proof which could explain an entire aspect of the universe in a few phrases. At the sight of his clean-shaven face, Esther had nodded then smiled, and tears had come into her eyes.

'Why are you crying?' Pierre had asked, taking her into his arms.

'I'm not,' she'd sniffed. 'I'm happy ... I'm getting you back.'

A few days later she had left to play a series of concerts in New York, and then his son had also departed for Les Arcs to go skiing with his friends. Pierre found himself alone for the days leading up to New Year. His wife had left him instructions as if he were a child. 'Make sure you get up in the morning.' Until relatively recently he had been known to sleep until one o'clock and drink his coffee in his dressing gown in front of Yves Mourousi and Marie-Laure Augry's lunchtime news programme.

'Don't be shy about asking Maria to make one of your favourite dishes, a *pot-au-feu* for example – that would be seasonal.' And she had especially reminded him not to forget his Friday session with Dr Fremenberg.

The large apartment on Avenue de Villiers was shrouded in silence, as always happened when Esther left on tour, but this time Éric wasn't there either. Not that they ever interacted much; a man of fifty-two doesn't often have a great deal to say to a fifteen -year-old boy and vice versa.

In a few years they would talk and exchange views on a variety of subjects, but, for the moment, Éric reserved for his parents that taciturn air of teenagers the world over that hinted at jollity and laughter with unknown friends.

'Our housekeeper told me that I look ten years younger,' Aslan went on in the silence. 'Which means I look forty-two, whereas, with my beard, I looked my age ... Or perhaps it means I looked sixty with my beard.'

'I would have said you looked sixty,' declared Fremenberg.

It was so rare for his psychoanalyst to speak that each time it happened Pierre felt his heart beat faster. Once he'd got over that, he turned towards his analyst.

'You thought I looked sixty?' he asked drily.

Fremenberg looked at him unblinkingly until Pierre looked away. And they didn't exchange another word for the whole of the rest of the session.

In the solitary days that followed, Pierre maintained his convalescent rhythm, rising at ten o'clock in order to shave with the greatest care. Then it was time for the television news with Yves Mourousi, followed by the lunch that Maria prepared for him. The rest of the day was happily spent reading magazines, or going out to buy various things like batteries for the remote control, spare light bulbs for the lamps, or new soles for his shoes.

The owner of Renovex, the chemist's on Rue de Levis, thought he was looking better and told him so. She also said that it was a good idea to get rid of the beard and that his hat was very elegant.

These unexpected compliments made him feel as if he had a new lease of life in the eyes of others. He was no longer that palely loitering and silent figure that no one ever spoke to. The subtle transformation had begun when he had started to wear a hat again. Wearing an accessory which recalled his glory days made him feel as if the old Pierre Aslan was reaching out to the disillusioned man he had become.

The felt hat was the only thing that he had taken possession of in a long time; it was something he had chosen, unless the hat had chosen him. Left on a bench, it could have been picked up by anyone. How long had it been there anyway? Even though he would never know who the official owner of the felt hat was, the mysterious F.M., from now on it was his hat.

The arrival of the hat in Pierre's life was responsible for a second change to his daily wardrobe. He discarded his old sheepskin jacket. One Sunday, after watching an episode of *Magnum* with an interest that surprised him, Pierre decided to go for a walk in the park. This broke his pattern of only going to the park on Friday before his appointment with Fremenberg.

It was so cold it felt as if it was about to snow; in fact Yves Mourousi had warned that it would probably do so on Monday. He walked with his hands in his pockets and the hat on his head. The park was almost deserted. The only people he passed were a pack of flushed joggers, jaws clenched and all wearing Walkmans.

He was passing the roller-skating rink where reckless children raced round, hanging on to the handrail to stop themselves from falling, when he noticed *kérakac* – the smell of burning wood. He followed the smell to a part of the park that was out of bounds to the public. He saw a column of smoke rising behind a bush.

Pierre walked over and found a gardener burning dead

leaves and dry wood, turning them over with a pitchfork. The gardener looked at Pierre.

'You're not really supposed to be here,' he said.

'I'm sorry, it was the smell of burning wood that attracted me.'

'You like it too? Well, in that case, you can stay. There's no one here anyway, and tomorrow it's going to snow.'

'Are you sure?'

The gardener nodded and put his hand on his lower back. 'I can feel it here. It's my personal barometer.'

Then he used his fork to scoop up a pile of dead wood and throw it on the fire. The two men stood there lost in thought in front of the crackling fire with its white smoke rising in curling plumes.

'Can I ask you something?'

'Go ahead,' said the gardener.

'Could we burn my jacket on the fire?'

'Pardon?'

'My jacket, do you think it would burn?'

'Why do you want to burn your clothes?'

'Because … I need to.'

After handing over a 50-franc note and emptying his pockets, Pierre put his jacket on top of the wood. He was reminded of the Hindu ritual of burning bodies on a pyre until they were reduced to cinders.

The jacket was enveloped in smoke, which became denser and, as the first burning branches caught the material, the fire took hold. The gardener watched his strange visitor in between his spadefuls of dead leaves.

Pierre removed his hat and held it in both hands at knee-height while he watched the flames do their work on the coat he'd worn for six winters.

When he returned to his flat, he opened the bedroom wardrobe looking for his black Yves Saint Laurent suit, but he couldn't find it. He had probably given it away with the others to the Salvation Army. But he found another suit, a charcoal-grey Lanvin, that seemed to have survived the great purge. Perhaps Esther had kept it, without telling him.

On one of the high shelves he discovered a white shirt he hadn't worn for years. And in his chest of drawers he found gold and mother-of-pearl cuff links. Pierre undressed, throwing his jeans onto the velvet armchair in a ball, and put on the suit trousers, the shirt and then the jacket. It took him a minute to wrestle the cuff links in. He looked at himself in the mirror on the inside door of the wardrobe, beardless in a suit and white shirt. The suit was a little tight at the waist but it didn't matter.

He closed the wardrobe door, walked through the apartment, put on his hat and went out.

Could he do it? It was so many years since he had undertaken this exercise. The last time, in spring 1982, he had tried it during a walk from the entrance of the Tuileries to the Arc de Triomphe du Carrousel, all the way through the gardens from west to east until he arrived in front of the Louvre.

He had then sat on a bench in the little square where several years later they would erect a glass and steel pyramid and thought, I'm finished. I couldn't identify at least a quarter of the perfumes I passed.

The challenge he now set himself had been a spur-of-the-moment decision. But he felt up to it. He was going to identify the perfumes of all the people he walked past in the street. Pierre breathed deeply then closed his eyes.

He counted backwards like a hypnotist bringing his subject back to reality: five, four, three, two … one, then he clicked his fingers and opened his eyes, stroked the brim of his hat and began to walk in a straight line. The rule of the exercise was that he mustn't stop or turn his head. A dark-haired woman with a bob was coming towards him in a black suit and Emmanuelle Khanh glasses. She was level with him and now she'd passed him. One second, two: the little gust of air that accompanied all movement swept over Pierre; 'Fidji,' he murmured.

Without slowing down at all, he waited for the man with the briefcase to pass him. The man wore a grey-checked suit and his hair was tied back in a ponytail. The two regulation seconds preceded the olfactory waft; Paco Rabanne pour Homme.

Now there was a group of three women in their thirties coming towards him. According to his self-imposed rules, although he wasn't allowed to stop or turn to look at anyone, he could cut across them.

'Oh, excuse me,' he said as he forced them to separate to get past him.

He brushed lightly against the one with mid-length brown hair (First by Van Cleef & Arpels), her friend's long blonde ponytail skimmed his jacket (L'Air du Temps) and as he passed the third, a petite blonde with short hair (Eau de Rochas), he heard her murmur, 'He's crazy, that man.'

Hat-trick, thought Pierre just as a young woman in jeans and a red beret hurried towards him; Poison.

A man in velvet trousers and a suede jacket walked diagonally in front of him cleaning his glasses; he wasn't wearing any cologne. There was just an odour of aftershave containing honeysuckle and mint mixed with cigarettes.

As he waited at the red light, Pierre found himself next to a runner who was jogging on the spot; sweat of course, but also Eau Sauvage. On the other side of the boulevard, he passed a couple in their fifties – probably tourists – who were trying to find where they were on a map; the woman wore Shalimar and the man smelt of Elnett hairspray. He steals his wife's hairspray, was Pierre's conclusion but he didn't have time to dwell on that before he detected Arpège on a woman with plaits wearing a grey trouser suit, then Habanita on a young blonde woman with blue eyes.

After that he had several Poison, another L'Air du Temps, two Solstice, then Lacoste for men, Montana by Montana, Quartz by Molineux, Anaïs Anaïs, Caron's Poivre, Yves Saint Laurent Rive Gauche, Sikkim by Lancôme, Joy, and a surprising Épilogue by Coryse Salomé.

When he reached Place Saint-Augustin, he sat down on a bench and took off his glasses and hat. His head was spinning. He had done it. A waiter from one of the cafés came over from his terrace to ask if he was all right.

'Drakkar Noir, Guy Laroche,' replied Pierre.

The snow was beginning to come down, in sparse flakes at first, then in flurries. He returned home soaked through, his hat covered in white powder. He tapped it so that the crystals fell off, and put it on the sitting-room radiator to dry.

On 18 April 1982, he had put down his smelling strips, stopped up the last five perfume bottles he'd opened and put them back in their places in the perfume organ. Then he'd left the room, locked the door and flung the key into the top drawer of the chest before getting drunk on '67 Bowmore. It was finished. His symbolic locking of the room was intended to put an end to twenty years of creativity.

No one dared touch the key; the orders were clear: the door must not be opened, the 'study' had been condemned. Not to be opened under any circumstances, not even for hoovering. The room became the tomb of his creative genius, a Bluebeard's chamber in which his perfume organ slept.

Aslan had designed the organ himself, a semicircular case with adjustable shelves on which almost three hundred bottles of essential oils were stored. It had taken the master carpenter in Faubourg Saint-Antoine nearly a year and a half to build it, using the best-quality wood. It was decorated with a mermaid created by a sculptor. The mythical fish-tailed creature had her left hand on her heart and in her other hand she held – over her head like a crown – a representation of his three-branched smelling-strip-holder.

She was Aslan's crest, his emblem, the muse that appeared on his letterhead and on the seal he used on his envelopes.

He planned to spend New Year's Eve on his own. Esther and Éric had phoned earlier, and in the evening Pierre settled down to while away the last hours of the year in front of the television, watching the highlights of the most important events of the last twelve months.

January – Thierry Sabine and Daniel Balavoine had been killed in the Paris–Dakar race, and the space shuttle *Challenger* exploded live on air a few minutes after it took off.

March – Jacques Chirac became prime minister, inaugurating the first ever cohabitation in French political history, and a bomb exploded in Galerie Point Show on the Champs-Élysées, killing two and injuring twenty-nine.

April – a reactor exploded at the nuclear plant in Chernobyl, but, thanks to an anticyclone, the radioactive cloud avoided France.

June – stand-up star Coluche died in a motorcycle accident on a minor road in the South of France.

September – terrorist attacks devastated the capital, targeting the main post office at Hôtel de Ville, a pub owned by Renault, the police headquarters on Île de la Cité, and Rue de Rennes.

November – Action Directe assassinated the head of state-owned Renault, Georges Besse, at point-blank range outside his house. That same month, TV impressionist Thierry Le Luron also died.

And this evening, 31 December, the French taken hostage in Lebanon, Marcel Carton, Marcel Fontaine, Jean-Paul Kaufmann and Jean-Louis Normandin, had still not been freed.

Aslan fetched some champagne, a dry Canard-Duchêne, the official supplier to the higher echelons of the army, popped the cork and poured himself a glass. He saluted the television with it and, as was his habit – one which caused Esther to roll her eyes – declaimed the motto of the French cavalry: 'To our wives! Our horses! And those who ride them!'

As he swallowed the first fizzy mouthful, the television showed the illuminated courtyard of the Élysée Palace at night. Classical music played and 'Best wishes from François Mitterrand, President of the Republic' appeared on the screen in yellow letters.

The image then faded gracefully away and the head of state appeared, sitting at his desk in front of the gilt of the Élysée Palace, the French flag in the background and a very beautiful golden inkwell in the foreground.

'My dear compatriots, I am grateful to the tradition that allows me for the sixth time to wish you a Happy New Year' – at that moment the camera zoomed slowly in on the President – 'and to send, in your name, expressions of friendship to those living in hardship from poverty, unemployment, illness, solitude or from the long anguishing wait for the return of a loved one. The good wishes I send you are the same as always,' he went on with easy charm: 'that France unites when it is important, that France protects and develops its democracy, that she survives the challenges of the modern world.

'The events of 1986 have shown how crucial it is to stand together without faltering against terrorist threats; they have shown that more than ever we must work to reduce unemployment; they have shown we must ...'

The President's voice was gradually lost to Pierre as a thought took shape. He was no longer listening. As he remained immobile on the sofa, his eyes were running slowly round the room. Vanilla and *kérakac* ... but also jasmine. He looked up and closed his eyes ... sweet myrrh ... but also the subtlety of leather ... a new perfume hung in the air. A combination of scents that corresponded to nothing known. It was incredibly subtle for a smell found in an apartment, an unusual coming together of notes which were balancing and adjusting themselves with each passing second.

Pierre opened his eyes. The perfume wasn't in his head, it was here in the room. He turned towards the radiator. The hat was drying on the heat of the metal. That was what it was.

He rose slowly and carefully so as not to disturb a single molecule of air and approached softly. The Eau d'Hadrien and Solstice had mingled in the moisture of the snow and drawn in a hint of burning wood from Parc Monceau.

'My dear compatriots, when I see what so many French men and women are capable of, in so many spheres, leaders in the fields of science, the arts, industry and sport, when I see the quality of our workers, our managers, our farmers, when I look at the role that France has played in international affairs, I am sure that we have everything it takes to succeed. All we need to add is the determination to succeed, and to do it together. Happy New Year, long live the Republic, long live France!'

The three smells were mingling and complementing each other in the heat. The perfect fusion, the ideal marriage. Pierre held his breath, then brought his face close to the hat. Time stood still. When it happened he thought he would faint. Sublime, divine, the perfect equilibrium between Solstice, Eau d'Hadrien and burning wood. A new fragrance of pure perfection. Angel's essence.

Aslan's hands began to tremble. He had not felt this for eight years. His secret muse was smiling on him again in the last few moments of the year. He closed his eyes and breathed deeply so that the intangible mixture entered his body, reached his blood, filled his veins, combined with his blood cells, then revived his whole being and reactivated the sleeping circuits of the Library of Alexandria that existed within him, the one that had burnt down one evening in the late seventies, taking with it the creative genius of Pierre Aslan.

The walls of the apartment seemed to disappear, then the paintings, the carpet, the television, the floorboards, the building, the block of houses, the *quartier*, the cars, the people, the pavements, the city and even the snow. Everything gone. There was nothing any more. No 1986, no hours, no minutes.

With staring eyes, Pierre saw nothing more than lists of thousands of names scrolling past: doses and flowers, roots and powders, alcohols and distillations, then a formula, pure, clear and as powerful as the one that describes a nuclear reaction. It was the formula for a perfume, two lines that would come to define the age, fashion and women.

His hands were trembling as he put the key in the lock. Pierre placed the hat on top of the perfume organ as though it were an ancient relic from the beginning of time. He sat down in his wide black leather armchair, raised haggard eyes to the mermaid, then reached out his hand to his sampling-strip-holder, and blew on it to clear the dust.

When they received the package, the men in grey seated in the large room with bay windows said nothing. It had been such a long time since they had seen that mermaid seal with the crown above her head. Aslan had given no sign of life for a good while. Three years? Six years? One man shrugged his shoulders, indicating that he couldn't remember either …

'He doesn't even ring us now, he uses the post,' said another man, visibly annoyed.

A man with grey hair opened the wax seal, and little splinters of wax fell on the glass of the conference table. Then he opened the box. It contained a bottle, also sealed and displayed on a little velvet cushion. There was no note, no letter of explanation, no formula. The man with grey hair picked up a steel paper knife bearing the logo of the famous brand and tapped the top of the bottle. New little flakes joined the others. Everyone gathered round as he opened the bottle.

He closed his eyes, then in a strange ritual gesture

presented it for the five men and three women around him to sniff. No one said anything for a long moment. Then they looked at each other and an electric current passed through the room as surely as if a charge of 12,000 volts had been released.

'Call him,' said the grey-haired man softly. 'Quickly!' he added. 'Before he offers it to Chanel or Saint Laurent.'

Then he looked at the bottle in the light and smiled the smile of a businessman who has to place himself in the hands of artists and can't quite believe it when the artists deliver. It was miraculous to him that all the millions of francs that would be invested in this perfume, its manufacture, its bottles, the whole industrial and financial process and even the price of the stock could all be the result of the imaginings of one man. The result of an idea that had occurred to the man one morning.

That was the great mystery of industry and of finance, that it all came from something intangible, insubstantial, almost mystical …

The white-aproned waiter had walked ahead of them down the line of tables where couples, families and tourists sat chatting, smiling or nodding their heads, their mouths full. Along the way, Aslan spotted seafood platters, entrecôte steaks with *pommes vapeur*, *faux-filets* with Béarnaise sauce.

A few days after signing the contract for his new fragrance, Pierre had decided to take his wife and son out to dinner. When they came in the head waiter, a man with crew-cut grey hair, had asked them if they'd booked, and then looked for the name Aslan on his list.

'Allow us to show you to your table,' he said, nodding to a waiter, who immediately hurried over.

They opened the red leatherette menu and began to read. The *plateau royal de fruits de mer* (3 people) was framed in the middle of the page, in elegant calligraphy: *fines de claire gillardeau*, a crab, two types of clam, langoustines, whelks, sea violets, sea urchins, prawns and winkles. Aslan took the wine list and looked for a Chevalier-Montrachet.

'Excellent choice ... Monsieur,' said the wine waiter, abandoning the time-honoured condescension to customers.

A few minutes later, he returned with the bottle, took hold of the corkscrew and performed the ritual opening, passing the cork under his nose. Aslan tasted the first mouthful and nodded. The wine waiter gave an approving nod in return, filled their glasses and departed. Aslan noticed that a few people were glancing at their table, probably music lovers who had recognised Esther.

'It must be Fremenberg who's cured you,' she said. 'Perhaps you shouldn't have stopped his sessions so suddenly.'

'Yes, I should,' Pierre protested lightly.

There had been no more sessions since the evening Pierre had opened the study door and sat down in front of his perfume organ. The following Friday, he had told Esther he was too busy to go to see Fremenberg.

'But, Pierre,' she had replied, horrified, 'you haven't missed a session in six years.'

To avoid any further discussion, which would have interrupted his work, Aslan had gone over to her, looked at her in silence then planted a kiss on her forehead, and, without a word, sat back down in his chair. Esther had left him alone.

The next week he had missed his appointment because there had been a test distillation at the laboratory at the very time he should have been at his analyst. And on the following Fridays Aslan was not to be found crossing Parc Monceau.

One morning he received a phone call from an unknown secretary telling him that he hadn't shown up for his appointments with Fremenberg for four months. If he wished to continue treatment, he would have to pay for all the missed appointments, the woman's voice informed him.

Pierre did not particularly like Fremenberg, and he liked even less the attitude that demanded that you pay for a service you hadn't received. It was highly questionable.

On the one hand it was fair enough that you should have to make reparation for the inconvenience of a missed appointment, but on the other hand, when you forgot to cancel a dinner reservation, you wouldn't be expected to pay for two meals when you next went to the restaurant.

What exactly did he owe Fremenberg? Nothing. The long silent sessions he had attended for six years had not helped him. It was the hat that had pulled him out of his depression. Had he not picked it up, nothing would have changed.

Pierre had developed a theory about all this, according to which he had a 'parallel life' where he had not taken the hat from the bench in Parc Monceau, his wife had not made that comment about his beard, he hadn't shaved it off, and of course the hat had not been placed on the sitting-room radiator on New Year's Eve.

In this 'parallel life' he was still wearing his old sheepskin jacket and had his beard, had never opened the door of his study and still went every Friday to his analyst. What Aslan called a 'parallel life' was actually a perfect illustration of quantum mechanics and of applied developments in probability theory, starting from the hypothesis that everything we do in our lives creates a new universe which does not in any way wipe out the previous universe.

Our lives can be thought of as like a tree hiding a forest of parallel lives in which we aren't exactly the same, nor are we wholly different. In certain of those lives, we wouldn't have married the same person, or lived in the same place, or had the same profession … To deny that Fremenberg had played any part in his recovery had one flaw: namely that without the weekly appointment with his analyst he would never have sat on the bench beside the hat.

So Pierre decided to work out the cost of the missed Friday appointments and send off a cheque for what he owed. He did not receive any response, but his cheque number 4567YL was cashed the next day.

'What do you think of the wine?' he asked his wife and son seriously.

'It's excellent,' replied Esther, and Éric voted it 'cool'.

A few moments later, a waiter placed a round stand in the middle of the table, a sign that the seafood platter was about to arrive. Next came a basket of pumpernickel bread, a ramekin of shallot vinaigrette, and the butter dish.

Aslan buttered a piece of bread and dipped it discreetly in the vinaigrette. Éric immediately followed suit and Esther frowned. The platter arrived, the seafood arranged by species on a bed of crushed ice.

Aslan took an oyster, held a quarter of lemon immediately above it, and squeezed gently. A drop of lemon juice fell onto the delicate membrane, which squirmed immediately.

The young cloakroom attendant gave him his hat and helped him on with his overcoat, then placed Esther's silk chiffon scarf over her shoulders, staring at her a little too fixedly.

'I was at Salle Pleyel … at your concert in March,' she whispered. 'The Prelude and Fugue in A minor was … unforgettable.'

'Thank you,' replied Esther with an embarrassed smile. She was always a little uncomfortable in the face of admiring comments. It was the only time that Aslan saw a trace of shyness pass over his wife's face.

'I'm touched, really,' she added, taking the hand of the young girl, who blushed.

Pierre slipped her a ten-franc piece and she gave him a brief smile, but it was Esther she couldn't take her eyes off. And no doubt she continued to look at her until the trio disappeared into the night.

In the taxi, Pierre, Éric and Esther squashed up together in the back because the passenger seat was occupied by a little sheepdog. Women taxi-drivers were quite rare, especially at night, and the dog must have been there for company and possibly for protection. Aslan was smiling as he watched the city pass. His son took the black hat from his knees where it had rested since they set off.

'Who is B.L.?'

'Sorry?'

'B.L., the initials in your hat, that's not you.'

'Your father bought it second hand.'

Aslan gently took the hat from his son and looked at the band of leather inside. It was the same make of black hat, and the letters were embossed in gold in the same place, but they weren't the same letters. Two men with identical hats in the same restaurant. The cloakroom attendant had made a mistake.

Cher Monsieur,

Before I go any further and risk raising your hopes, let me make it clear from the outset that I cannot return the item you appeal for in your advert. It's out of my hands. Nonetheless, I wanted to write to you because the hat you are looking for means something to me too: I wore it for almost twenty-four hours. One evening, one morning and one afternoon, to be exact.

You mention the Paris–Le Havre 06781 train in your advert, but it had a different number by the time I took it on its return journey (mine was the 67854 service). I got on at Le Havre at 9.25 p.m. on the same day you lost your hat, so it must have been yours I found on the luggage rack opposite seat number 88. I only noticed it as we were pulling in to Paris. Since it was raining, I picked it up and put it on. This one small action was to change my life. The leather band inside your lovely black felt hat happens to be embossed with my very own initials. I took this as a good omen, like a kind of lucky charm to carry with me.

The story I am about to tell you is of a somewhat personal nature, and I hope you will not be uncomfortable reading it. The night I picked up your hat, I was on my way to meet a man. One of many such meetings, I should point out. Please don't get the wrong idea: I don't have legions of admirers, and I certainly don't trade on my charms! I say many, because this was by no means the first time I had gone to meet this man. That night's date was set to be just like the one before it, and the ones before that, and so on.

For more than two years, I had been having an affair with a married man who continually promised he would leave his wife for me but never went through with it … I had suspected for some time that we probably had no future together and that the more dates I filled up my diary with, the closer we were getting to the end. It is in the nature of an affair not to last; its ephemeral quality is what makes it so attractive, and trying to keep it going often leads to nothing but disappointment and disillusion. Forgive me, I'm rambling.

It was your hat, that night in Batignolles – where we always met, because of its proximity to Gare Saint-Lazare and the abundance of cheap hotels – that sealed the end of my relationship with Édouard and allowed me to see that, when all was said and done, he didn't really care for me. I won't go into the details of our break-up here, since you can read them at your leisure (should you wish) in my short story 'The Hat', which I'm enclosing, photocopied from the March edition of *Ouest-France*. Everything in it is true to life, from the events to the places where they happened.

So Édouard disappeared from my life with the help of your hat. And I really mean disappeared, because I've heard nothing at all from him since. In the days following our split, I kept checking my answerphone, hoping he might change his mind or at least come back for a better explanation. Nothing. To this day, I haven't heard another word from Édouard and I don't suppose I ever will.

Thanks to your hat, I also wrote the story that won me the very prestigious Prix Balbec. You may not have heard of it, but it's awarded every two years on the spring equinox in the Cabourg hotel immortalised by Marcel Proust. The jury was made up of local dignitaries, authors and journalists. Amid the crowd of people gathered round the champagne and trays of canapés, one man instantly stood out.

He had grey hair, white around the temples, was smartly dressed in a pearl-grey suit and, above all, was holding a felt hat in the same colour. My recent experience of hats immediately drew my attention to the only one present that evening.

I had been lying when I told Édouard I was seeing an older man who wore a hat and had given me one like it. It may seem strange to you, but this is not the first time one of my stories has come true. Indeed, I wrote 'Change of Address' (awarded third place in the 'Many Words, One Town' competition, 1984) four months before I actually moved house; and I firmly believe that 'An Afternoon at the Harbour' (recited at Le Havre Theatre Festival 1985), about a young woman sitting in a café awaiting the return of her husband, a captain in the merchant navy, prefigured my own brief fling with a fisherman, since six months later I found myself in that woman's place, sitting in a café waiting for him.

This time, the character of the older man with the hat had come to me out of nowhere and yet, since the prize ceremony, I must admit he has become an important part of my life, and that my life is changing.

I'm not sure I will stick around in Le Havre much longer, and I'm not sure I'll stay in my job either. No, I'm not hoping to become a writer – it's too hard to make a career out of, and I don't have the talent or drive to succeed – but I've been thinking about setting up a bookshop ...

There's a lovely shop going on one of the main streets in Cabourg and the more I think about it, the more I can see myself as a bookseller. Michel (that's what my man in the grey hat is called) has offered to buy it for me.

He has also offered to start a new life with me and marry me. This time, it's me who isn't sure. Everything has happened so quickly.

If you hadn't left your hat on the train that day, my life would still be exactly the same and I would no doubt be waiting for my next date in Batignolles.

Who knows why I've written you such a long letter. It must be because I have a man in my life who wears a hat; I feel the need to confide in another man with a hat, who set this all in motion. Sadly, the ending of my story is exactly as it happened. I no longer have your hat. I'm afraid I can't tell you any more.

I wish you all the very best and sincerely hope you find what you are looking for.

Fanny Marquant

Daniel Mercier
8 Rue Henri Le Secq des Tournelles
76000 Rouen

Mademoiselle,

Your letter took me by surprise. Firstly because I was no longer expecting a reply to my notice in the paper. In fact, I was planning to cancel it when I received your message, forwarded to me by the newspaper's classified section. I'm absolutely certain it was my hat you picked up on the train.

I have read your story several times and congratulate you on your writing style, and on winning the Prix Balbec. Your account of the day and a half you spent with my hat has affected me deeply and only confirmed what I already knew from experience: this is no ordinary hat. As you have confided in me in your letter I shall do the same. It will do me good, since work has been very stressful recently.

Believe me when I tell you, Mademoiselle, that the hat has changed my life, too. I would not be in my present post nor would I be living in the beautiful city of Rouen had it not crossed my path. My name is Daniel Mercier: those are not my initials on the hat, but it is indeed mine, and it remains of great importance to me for reasons I cannot go into here. I was so attached to it that when I lost it, I suffered a recurrence of dyshidrotic eczema for the first time in fifteen years. I consulted my doctor, who asked if I had experienced 'a major setback or frustration'.

When I replied that I had lost my hat, he didn't feel that this was a sufficiently 'frustrating' setback to lead to a flare-up of a past skin condition. I stopped seeing him after that, and have since consulted Dr Gonpart, a senior registrar trained at the very best hospitals, who shares my view on the link between stress and dyshidrotic eczema, having observed similar attacks in patients suffering from shock. In particular, he highlighted the case of a man who had come up in blotches minutes after losing his wedding ring in the sea.

But I digress, Mademoiselle, and will bore you no further with my ailments, which have since been most effectively treated.

Your very fine story, 'The Hat', is, for me, the epilogue to a very personal encounter with our black Homburg. You tell me that the end of your story is true. There is, then, no hope.

How can I begin to track down the bearded man in the sheepskin jacket, who picked it up off the bench in Parc Monceau?

I understand your wish to keep your story as true to the facts as possible, but still I find it hard to believe you really left the hat there. In an ideal world, you would have remained in possession of the hat, read my notice and been able to return it to me.

Sadly, we do not live in an ideal world, and the irony of it is that the prize money for the Prix Balbec (3,000 francs) is precisely the sum I was planning to offer as a reward to whoever returned my hat.

I hope you will find happiness with the other 'man in the hat' – the grey one – and in your new venture in the charming town of Cabourg, which I have not yet visited. I passed your story on to my wife, who was deeply touched by your writing and asks me to ask you where she might purchase your two other stories – 'An Afternoon at the Harbour' and 'Change of Address'.

With best regards,

Daniel Mercier

Monsieur,

I was very touched by the letter you sent by return and I completely understand how the loss of something so precious can cause all kinds of distress, as you have suffered with your eczema. I really am sorry for leaving the hat in Parc Monceau. It was a rather irrational thing to do; I was carried away by my writing, and I too came to regret it in the weeks that followed. I was very fond of that hat, and when I looked into buying myself another, I realised I could never afford one.

By way of apology, and for the benefit of your wife, I am enclosing the manuscripts of all three of my short stories. None of them have been published, so you won't find them in any bookshop. I hope you both enjoy reading them, and wish you every happiness.

Fanny Marquant

Mademoiselle,

I thoroughly enjoyed reading more of your work. Your style and characters are so engaging. My favourite has to be 'An Afternoon at the Harbour' – I really identified with the woman waiting for her husband at the Café des Deux Mouettes, thinking about her life now, in the past and in the years to come. I think a lot of women would see themselves in the character of Murielle. Well done and thank you for moving me with your writing.

Véronique Mercier

PS What a shame you couldn't get my husband's hat back. He talks of nothing else!

Librairie de la Mouette
Fanny Marquant – Bookseller
17 Rue Marcel-Proust
14390 Cabourg

Monsieur,

We were briefly in touch a few months ago on the subject of the hat you lost on the Paris–Le Havre train.

I wanted to get this article to you as quickly as possible. I ripped it out of a magazine at the hairdresser's just this morning.

It's an interview which appeared in *Paris Match* a fortnight ago. At first glance, the man in the picture wasn't familiar, but when I saw that he had created Solstice, the perfume I wear myself, I read on and was amazed.

You'll see what I mean when you read his answer to the question at the bottom left of page 46. I turned back to look at the photo again and asked the hairdresser to lend me a biro so I could draw a beard on his clean-shaven face. I had seen those round glasses before.

Then I remembered something else I didn't put in my story: he smelt the hat before taking it with him. Monsieur Mercier, the man who picked up the hat and the man you see on the two pages I enclose are one and the same person.

Kindest regards,

Fanny Marquant

PS The hairdresser's biro was blue, which has made him look strangely like Bluebeard …

THE SIXTH SENSE

Exclusive interview with 'nose' Pierre Aslan.
Words: Mélaine Gaultier
Pictures: Marianne Rosenstiehl

*Described as the Stanley Kubrick of the perfume world, French
'nose' Pierre Aslan is back with a new fragrance which already
promises to be one of the defining scents of the decade. We
meet the legendary creator of Solstice and Sheraȝ.*

*We left you on the woody notes of Alba, back in the late 1970s.
How would you sum up this decade's fragrance?*
Like the women of today, of whom you are a great example:
beguiling, free, independent, with just a suggestion of
animal passion, totally modern, captivating ... perhaps
even captivated?

By you? No doubt about it, Monsieur Aslan.
Oh but I do doubt it! [Laughs.] Men are always full of
doubt, which is why they make perfumes: so they can give
them to you and win you over.

How has your style developed over the years?
It's difficult to say ... A perfume should be representative
of its era, and yet able to transcend it. It's the women who
wear it that bring it to life and develop it. Take Habanita,

for example. It was created in 1921, and today in 1987, many women still wear it. They approach it differently, and wear it differently too.

How do you mean?
Women have changed, so perfume has changed too ...

In what way have they changed?
Their skin is different. The species has evolved: the skin of a girl of the eighties is nothing like the skin of a girl in the 1920s. She doesn't use the same soap, or the same face powder; the washing powder she uses to clean her bed linen is completely different. The smell of the city itself has changed beyond all recognition. The humidity of the atmosphere too. A woman in the court of Louis XV would smell nothing like a woman today, and it's not about what perfume she's wearing. It's to do with her skin.

So skin changes with the times?
Absolutely. Think of the eighteenth century. What does that era smell like? Stone, sunshine, wood, manure, leaves, wrought iron. Nowadays it's petrol, tarmac, metallic paint, plastic ... electricity.

Electricity has a smell?
Of course. So do TV screens.

What made you go back to perfume-making after an eight-year gap?
It was finding a hat ... on a bench in Parc Monceau.

I don't understand ...
It doesn't matter. It's too complicated to explain. Let's move on.

Monsieur,

Your letter concerning my interview with Pierre Aslan was forwarded to me by the *Paris Match* editorial office. I must say I found it very intriguing. I'm just starting out as a journalist and yours is the first item of correspondence I have received – and it's not one I'm likely to forget in a hurry.

To tell the truth, the only reason I got the exclusive with Pierre Aslan was that my little sister is in the same class as Monsieur Aslan's son. Éric fancies my sister and I think the interview served as a way of getting closer to her … Pierre Aslan hadn't given a single interview in thirteen years, so I was a quivering wreck when I went to meet him.

Coming back to your letter, are you quite sure that the hat you left on the bench in Parc Monceau is the same one Monsieur Aslan describes? Personally, I was baffled by his answer – I still am, in fact. I actually thought that section might be cut, but the editor wanted to keep it in because it shows what a complex and disconcerting character Pierre Aslan is.

As for your request, I'm sorry but I can't give you Monsieur Aslan's home address. I didn't meet him at his house but in the bar at the Ritz with his publicist, and, in any case, even if I had his address I wouldn't be allowed to give it to you. However, I am enclosing the contact details for his publicist; if you wish to write to Monsieur Aslan, I think you could go via him.

Wishing you every success with your search and all best wishes,

Mélaine Gaultier

ASLAN

Monsieur,

Your letter is one of the strangest I have ever received. The description of your hat corresponds in every detail to a black felt hat I picked up on a bench in Parc Monceau. In fact, I mentioned that very hat in the only interview I have given recently, in *Paris Match*. Alas! I no longer have the hat, which I regret, because I was very sentimentally attached to it. Life is like that; objects pass from hand to hand, but people and perfumes remain.

With best wishes,

Pierre Aslan

ASLAN

Monsieur,

My press secretary has again passed on a letter from you. As you are being so persistent, I will try to make my reply as clear as possible: I don't have your hat any more because I lost it in a brasserie. To be even more specific, that evening there was an unfortunate mix-up. The cloakroom attendant gave me back a hat that was identical to yours in every particular, except that the golden initials were not F.M., they were B.L. I only noticed this when it was too late. I went back to the brasserie the next day but the hat was no longer there.

I hope that I have enlightened you sufficiently in this matter and I would ask you not to write to me again. I like my solitude, very rarely answer the telephone and almost never reply to letters.

Yours sincerely,

Pierre Aslan

ASLAN

Monsieur,

Please find enclosed the answer to your third request, the address of the brasserie where I lost the hat that means so much to you, along with details of the exact date and time of the loss. This now concludes our correspondence once and for all.

You will also find enclosed a bottle of my latest creation which you may offer to the woman of your choice. This letter requires no response.

Aslan

Bernard Lavallière slammed the door of his Peugeot 505. The dinner had gone badly and his wife had not said a word to him since their bust-up in the car. Pierre and Marie-Laure de Vaunoy had invited them to their apartment on the Champ-de-Mars, along with three other couples. It should have been like any other dinner party, when you expect at least to relish the conversation, if not what's on the menu.

The food is always terrible in town, especially amongst the aristocracy. The upper classes might get out the family china and crested silverware, but they very often take a perverse pleasure in serving food the cobbler or the concierge would turn their nose up at.

The only way to get a decent dinner is to eat with the people, Bernard liked to say; not that he had sat down to eat 'with the people' for several decades, but he cherished childhood memories of the housekeeper's cooking at the family estate in Beaune – memories he had no one to share with and which from time to time, when the meal in front of him was really too awful to stomach, he felt he could almost taste again.

Yet the evening's drama could not wholly be put down to the de Vaunoys' cooking. 'It is worse than a crime, Sire, it's a mistake,' Antoine Boulay de la Meurthe had said to Napoleon on learning of the execution of the Duc d'Enghien in the moat at Vincennes. Bernard Lavallière hadn't put anyone in front of a firing squad, but his mistake had rung out like a gunshot in the middle of the meal.

It all began with a glass of champagne – just the one, and distinctly mediocre – served with dry crackers the hostess was eager to point out had been bought on the cheap from Félix Potin.

The guests had arrived punctually, a few at a time. They rang the doorbell to be greeted by cries of 'Ah, here they are! Do come in!' or 'Why, look who it is! Come in, we've been longing to see you …' – the usual over-the-top exclamations hammed up further by Marie-Laure de Vaunoy's apparent amazement at finding each invitee on her doorstep, as though it were by some incredible coincidence that they had turned up there.

The ladies left their shawls and handbags in the entrance hall before making their way to the living room where the men were shaking hands and complaining about how long it had taken to find a parking space. The husbands who had arrived before them sympathised with resigned, manly sighs.

In the car on the way there, Bernard had already begun

to dread that they would once again have to endure the de Vaunoys' chicken with apricots. After a starter of cucumber and cream, the Spanish girl serving the food brought out a large silver platter. The fowl took pride of place in the centre of the dish, but was covered in a dubious-looking sauce and surrounded by shrivelled apricots. Bernard had a breast which turned out to be so dry it made him thirsty for the rest of the night.

Luckily, the wine was within reach. He intended to employ a straightforward technique: keep offering the bottle around to his neighbours so he could top himself up as often as he liked. The conversation hummed around the topic of visits to the theatre, cinema and concerts.

'We had dinner next to Esther Kerwitcz just last night,' said Charlotte Lavallière, certain of getting a reaction. She let the gasps die down before telling the story of visiting the splendid brasserie with a couple of friends and spotting the famous pianist just a few tables away, having dinner with her husband and son.

Marie-France Chastagnier was envious – what luck to have seen such a great artist close up! – and gushed as she recalled an Esther Kerwitcz concert at the Salle Pleyel three years earlier. Her husband made a face and declared he preferred Rubinstein, to which Marie-Laurence de Rochefort replied that Rubinstein didn't play Bach.

Jean-Patrick Le Baussier brought up the name Glenn Gould. Colonel Larnier stated matter-of-factly that all the great musicians were Jewish.

For his part, Gérard Peraunot pointed out that Esther

Kerwitcz was a very beautiful woman, earning him a furious glance from his wife, and then they moved on to talking about their children.

A variety of anecdotes about Scout and Brownie weekends ensued, and plans to make pilgrimages to Santiago de Compostela were shared. Everyone sang the praises of Father Humbert, who was so good with the children and whom they described deferentially as a holy man. (No one had any inkling that the clergyman would be arrested sixteen years later as part of a huge police operation which would uncover no less than 87,000 indecent images of children on the hard drive of his computer.)

The upbringing of their offspring led them on to the topic of television, root of all evil, a devilish device which did little more than hold a mirror up to their decadent society.

The presenter Stéphane Collaro was singled out for particular scorn: not content with dulling the brains of the nation's youth, his programme *Cocoboy* was also guilty of tainting Saturday nights with 'you know what' since it showed – or so they had been told – a girl performing a most risqué striptease.

The Larniers confessed to keeping their set solely for the purposes of watching *Apostrophes*. This weekly dose of culture left them with the impression that they had read every book discussed on the show. The colonel's wife thus felt quite entitled to give her opinion on any novel reviewed on *Apostrophes*, while adding that she had not actually got around to buying a copy. Serge Gainsbourg's appearance on the show the previous December, tanked up on Pastis 51 and Gitanes and treating a fellow guest like a peasant, had outraged the Larniers. They had seriously considered getting rid of their television, but the reassuring sight of a respectable writer on the following week's programme put that rash idea out of their heads.

The mere mention of Michel Polac provoked a chorus of indignation from the guests, but – thank goodness – the new owner of channel TF1 had just rid France of the shouting match that was *Droit de réponse*. Hubert and Frédérique de la Tour were struggling to follow all this, but they weren't sorry; they prided themselves on not owning a television.

Their steadfast refusal to purchase a set meant one whole French family had never heard of Michel Drucker; a permanent chat-show fixture, he could have been a fourth-century Hindu mathematician for all they knew. They knew exactly who the Mourousis were: an old aristocratic Phanariot Greek family originally from Mourousa, near Trabzon – but they had no idea that one of their number was the presenter of the one o'clock news.

They never went to the cinema either, and lived happily in a world of stills somewhere between the eras of Niépce and Nadar. Pierre de Vaunoy, as master of the house, found the one way to put an end to all the talk of television:

'What can I say? It's all down to the lefties ...'

'True,' chimed in Jean-Patrick Teraille, 'but this won't be the end of it. Just you wait: I'll bet you anything Mittrand stands again.'

'Can you please pronounce his name correctly.'

*

Bernard Lavallière spoke, then swallowed the last of his wine. By the time he put his glass down, silence had descended and everyone was staring at him.

'Mittrand', that contraction favoured by old-school, *vieille France* right-wingers, which hinted at more extreme views. And yet this was not the first time he had heard the word used; the seventh, sixteenth and eighth formed the leading triumvirate of Paris *arrondissements* in which it was regularly uttered at dinner parties. Staunch Gaullists, solid UDF centrists, closet Front National supporters and proud royalists joined forces to mispronounce the head of state's name with the unspoken purpose of marking themselves out as members of the same club.

'Mittrand' served as a password among them. This brotherhood of the right, ranging from the most respectable to the furthest fringes, delighted in breaking the rules of French pronunciation with their non-standard use of the silent 'e'. Bernard's unexpected, abrupt correction had left the dining room several degrees cooler. The chicken, already cold, seemed colder, the apricots yet more shrivelled and the glasses frosted.

Not even Bernard could have explained what had made

him come out with such a thing. The sentence had spoken itself. Was it the memory of those childhood lunches coming back to him as he chewed the revolting fowl? Could it be the fact that, unlike him, Jean-Patrick Teraille still owned his ancestral home in Poitou? Had he simply drunk too much wine? … No, it really was inexplicable.

'I've always called him Mittrand and I always will – if it's all the same to you, Bernard,' Jean-Patrick Teraille replied icily, while Colonel Larnier glared at him, clenching his jaw, as though presiding over a court martial for high treason.

'You haven't gone leftie on us, have you, old chap?' Pierre Chastagnier asked slyly.

'Batting for the other side now, are we?' chuckled Frédérique de la Tour.

Bernard felt something inside he could not put his finger on; a sensation of total peace and warmth was enveloping him, spreading all the way up his spine. It reached his neck, then his head, and a mysterious smile played on his lips.

'What exactly do you have against Mitterrand?' he asked softly. 'We're all sitting around this table the same way we did three years ago, six years ago, eight, ten, fifteen years ago. What difference has 10 May 1981 made to our lives?'

There was a long pause.

'Think about it,' said Bernard, 'it hasn't changed anything.'

'What about the communist government ministers!' cried Pierre Chastagnier.

'Indeed, what about them? The Communist Party is

dissolving like sugar in water. Mitterrand has achieved in the space of six years what the Right failed to do in thirty.'

'You're just playing devil's advocate!'

'Mitterrand is not the devil ... but he is an advocate,' Bernard said with a smile.

The heel of a Céline stiletto is a weapon too often overlooked by the male of the species, and a violent kick in the shin made him look up to meet Charlotte's livid gaze.

'He represents France to the rest of the world,' muttered Jean-Patrick Teraille, 'and I can't abide it!'

'What kind of image are we projecting with a socialist president?' threw in Hubert de la Tour.

'What kind of image?' repeated Bernard in surprise. 'Why, the very best,' he said, discreetly nursing his leg. 'Mitterrand is well liked wherever he goes. And as a result he has forged stronger relationships with his counterparts, whether it's Helmut Kohl, President Reagan, Gorbachev or Margaret Thatcher. He's popular in France too, people love him.'

'People? What people?!' fumed Hubert de la Tour.

'The people ...' replied Bernard, smiling.

'He's Machiavellian,' complained Pierre de Vaunoy.

'So he is,' said Bernard, grinning. 'You should re-read *The Prince*.'

'*The Prince?*'

'Machiavelli's *The Prince*. It's all in there.'

'As if you've ever read it,' Charlotte shot back coldly.

Bernard blinked imperceptibly. '"I will only conclude that a prince must have the people on his side, otherwise he will not have support in adverse times."'

'How enlightening ...'

Everyone turned to face Colonel Larnier, who had not slackened his jaw. He had just discovered in Bernard an object even more worthy of his wrath than the artist responsible for the reggae version of the 'Marseillaise'.

'Monsieur,' he went on, breathless with rage, 'I refuse to sit here listening to you eulogising François Mitterrand. The manner in which you cut Monsieur Teraille off was unspeakable. Once upon a time such quarrels were fought to the death!'

The lady of the house tried to calm the colonel down as he carried on mumbling about the voice of France, General de Gaulle and damned usurpers. Then silence descended, and, after a brief lull, the good manners common to the very best households were restored.

When the time came to take their leave, Bernard thanked his hosts and went to say goodbye to the other guests, while unbeknownst to him his wife was apologising profusely to the hostess.

In the hallway he put on his Burberry coat, helped Charlotte with her shawl and placed his black felt hat on his head, without noticing that the initials embossed inside had skipped a few places up the alphabet.

At half past midnight, as his wife was falling into a fitful sleep – in spite of taking a sleeping tablet – Bernard, alone in the living room, poured himself a cognac. No one had backed him up, even half-heartedly, when he had dared to ask for the President's name to be pronounced properly. And Charlotte had gone as far as to lay into his calf in the most underhand manner.

The initial mockery he met with had quickly given way to undisguised loathing. When they got up to leave, the colonel had looked Bernard up and down as he shook his hand with a contempt no one had shown him since he was in short trousers. *Once upon a time such quarrels were fought to the death.* A duel? Whatever next?

Bernard kicked himself for failing to think in time of a suitably cutting put-down. It had come to him in the lift: No need for that, my dear colonel, you're already brain-dead. Wonderful, it would have pierced the colonel's heart more effectively than the fastest bullet.

On the way home, his wife had thrown what could

easily be described as a fit of hysteria: 'We're going to fall out with all our friends, thanks to you!' she had shrieked.

'Our friends?'

Bernard finished his cognac in one gulp and poured another. What the hell? he thought to himself. Everyone's asleep, I can do what I like.

In what way did these people really count as friends? It was far too strong a word for what they meant to him; just because you had had the same sort of education, had gone to the same parties and the same universities, that didn't make you *friends*. It was ridiculous to think that it did. They moved in the same circles – that was all. Friendship was something else entirely; it was the stuff of great poets and writers.

The names Montaigne and La Boétie sprang to mind, but he swiftly brushed them aside; they were perhaps not the best example, since the close friendship between the two authors was rumoured to have gone as far as sodomy.

Saint-Exupéry, on the other hand, had written very eloquently on the subject, with his tale of the little tamed fox you were forever responsible for. The dinner party guests had been nothing like vulnerable little foxes; rather they resembled hyenas that had smelt blood the moment he had spoken.

That evening, in a matter of seconds, the well-respected man with the important job at AXA had become 'suspect'.

They eyed me as if I were their prey, Bernard reflected. They're all big hunters, after all, and I've always turned down their invitations to country meets. So what exactly do I have in common with these people? With this question, which he had never asked himself before, a chasm opened before him.

His stomach gurgled and an image of the chicken with apricots came back to him. He banished it, replacing it with the memory of Henriette at the stove.

Henriette lived in the little house at the entrance to the family estate, between Le Clos-des-Deux-Pies and the Rivaille property. The extended Lavallière family – parents, cousins, uncles and grandparents – came together in the big house several times a year during the school holidays.

Henriette, whose husband Bernard had never known because he had died twenty years earlier, shared the gatekeeper's cottage with her brother, Marcel. He made his living as an odd-job man, doing everything from gardening to masonry.

He had never been known to have a woman in his life and, many years later, it was rumoured that Marcel liked men, but that was never confirmed.

Being allowed inside Henriette's house was a privilege which was not afforded to all the Lavallière children. Some of them were judged to be too grown-up, others too little; the optimum age range was between seven and twelve.

The lunch to which the ten or so children were invited always began in the same way, with a walk around Henriette's vegetable patch. It was there that they learnt to recognise aromatic herbs and vegetables; sometimes they were even allowed to try them.

Marcel would take an Opinel knife out of his trouser

pocket and, in front of the fascinated children, would cut a carrot or tomato into little pieces and hand them round.

Afterwards, everyone sat down around the big table, always covered in the same red and white oilcloth. Henriette would stand at the coal-fired stove and the bowls would be filled with a *pot-au-feu* that would put most restaurants to shame. Sometimes they got a melt-in-the-mouth *blanquette*, ossobucco or cabbage with bacon instead – local dishes cooked from secret recipes that had been passed down through the generations, which none of these children's mothers could hope to recreate in their Paris kitchens. They had their cooks for that, of course, but none of them were a patch on Henriette.

Time had passed and after the death of Bernard's grandparents, the estate had been sold, savagely carved up among the inheritors. The warmth of that kitchen and the sweet aromas of his childhood had gone for good.

The guests at the dinner demonstrated perfectly why there had been latent hostility towards the middle and upper classes for centuries.

Giscard d'Estaing, that *grand bourgeois* made aristocratic by the title his forebears bought in 1922, but taken fully into the fold through marriage, was another fine example. What was it Mitterrand had said to him at the debate between the two rounds of the presidential elections? 'First of all, I don't appreciate your tone. I am not your pupil and you are not the President of the Republic here, you are merely my opponent.' His words struck a chord.

To think I voted for Giscard, mused Bernard, when

the word 'fossil' came to mind – the word that meant ancient sediments. 'That's exactly what they are, fossils,' he whispered to himself, slamming his glass down on the coffee table. Fossils, some of whom don't own a TV and are proud of the fact. Fossils, who wish nothing would ever change, living in their old apartments with the same old decor.

Bernard looked up and caught sight of the portrait of his ancestor Charles-Édouard Lavallière which had been hanging over the mantelpiece for two generations. It was to this man with grey sideburns and an imperial profile that his family still owed a large part of its fortune, held in apartments and office space in the capital – originally plots of land which his forebear had built on during the Haussmann-era redevelopment of Paris.

His gaze fell on the Louis XVI dresser and the two Ming vases sitting on top of it. He turned to the white marble mantelpiece and the Louis XVI gilt bronze carriage clock depicting Diana the huntress and a fawn. Then he looked round at the Louis XIII cabinet beside the window, the Laura Ashley drapes, the lace curtains, the six matching Louis XVI armchairs, the Persian rug, the Louis-Philippe stool and the desk of the same era.

On the walls there were landscape paintings from about 1800 depicting imaginary ruins peopled with unconvincing shepherdesses, and a rather kitsch pastel drawing of unclear provenance, showing a woman looking up at the sky as though faced with an apparition of the Virgin Mary. There was also an Aubusson tapestry on the opposite wall and a Charles X crystal chandelier.

Bernard realised with dismay that his apartment was decorated no differently from the homes of his fellow dinner party guests. Take the painting hanging above the sofa. It depicted a bucolic scene beside a babbling brook, with a church in the background.

A circular hole had been cut in the canvas where the bell tower was and a real enamel clock mechanism inserted. Its hands had fallen off at some point over the years; Bernard had never known it any other way. In theory, the picture was supposed to chime and give the time. It did nothing of the sort; it had not worked for decades. Bernard had inherited it from his father, who had inherited it from his father, and no one knew which Lavallière it had originally come from – it was just there, a permanent, useless object, and by the very presence of its handless clock face, it symbolised time standing still.

The disfigured canvas seemed to tell him: You're a conventional bourgeois and you always will be. You're exactly the same as everyone else at that dinner. Just like them, you live surrounded by things you did not choose and to which you have contributed almost nothing new. Your children will do the same and their children after them, and so it will go on.

You're nothing but a conservative, in every sense of the word. A product of your milieu, with nothing to distinguish you – just like your father, your grandfather and all the generations to come. You are not a man of your time; just look at that clock face – you don't even know what hour or year you're living in.

Bernard felt a sudden desire to read Machiavelli's *The*

Prince. 'As if you've ever read it,' Charlotte had had the audacity to snipe. Of course he had read it while studying law, but he had never so much as opened it since. The mere fact of being able to recite from it so accurately that evening should have earned him universal admiration.

He went into his study and scanned the shelves for a good fifteen minutes before laying his hands on the cheap paperback edition, whose pages were already yellowed. He opened it and read:

'A wise ruler cannot and should not keep his word when it would be to his disadvantage to do so, and when the reasons that made him give his word have disappeared. If all men were good, this rule would not stand. But as men are wicked and not prepared to keep their word to you, you have no need to keep your word to them.

'It is vital to understand that a prince, especially a new prince, cannot afford to cultivate attributes for which men are considered good. In order to maintain the State, a prince will often be compelled to work against what is merciful, loyal, humane, upright and scrupulous. He must have a spirit that can change depending on the winds and variations of Fortune, and, as I have said above, he must not, if he is able, distance himself from what is good, but must also, when necessary, know how to prefer what is bad.'

As he read these words, he felt a splitting headache come on and went to bed.

'... Are you sure?' the newsagent with the moustache asked doubtfully.

Every morning, Bernard was up with the lark and went out early to buy *Le Figaro*. He could have taken out a subscription, of course, but the outing had become part of his daily routine. Once he had bought the paper, he would head home to have breakfast with his family before setting off for the office. He had got to know three different newsagents over time and had a very good relationship with all of them. He was their quarter-to-seven customer, the one who always bought *Le Figaro*, plus the *Madame* and *Magazine* supplements at the weekend.

'Yes, I'm sure,' replied Bernard evenly.

For the first time in the thirteen years he had been running the kiosk at Passy, Marcel Chevasson had just sold a copy of '*Libé*' to his morning customer. This sort of thing never happened.

Customers fell strictly into one of two categories: the fickle ones, who picked up a newspaper and cleared off never to be seen again, and the unswervingly loyal. This kind of customer shared an understanding with his newsagent, the soul of discretion, who never dreamt of commenting or passing judgement on his purchases.

Thus every Thursday Chevasson served his two regular buyers of Jean-Marie Le Pen's rag, *National Hebdo*: a thirty-something skinhead and an elderly gentleman with a walking stick, Loden coat and gloves in winter.

The same went for the porn mags. *Union* and *Lui* readers purchased their magazines discreetly but without shame, and Marcel Chevasson handed them over as disinterestedly as if they were copies of *Le Point* or *Valeurs Actuelles*.

What would happen if the old man with the stick started buying *Le Figaro*? What if the skinhead asked for *L'Équipe*, or the smutty-picture lovers switched to *France-Dimanche* or *Point de Vue*? The *Figaro* man had just upset a delicate balance and Marcel Chevasson was thrown off kilter for the rest of the morning.

Peering over the stack of gossip magazines, he realised the changes did not stop there. His customer had not walked back towards his street as he usually did but, still wearing his hat, had sat down at a pavement café to read '*Libé*' while sipping a café crème.

More precisely – though Marcel Chevasson could not see this – he was savouring a scathing piece on Jacques Chirac. Terribly well written and vicious as you like, the article pulled apart every one of the Prime Minister's mistakes since coming to office.

A quarter of an hour later, Bernard passed through the

entrance hall of his apartment building. The concierge did a double take; no, she had not imagined it, it really was Monsieur Lavallière who had just walked past her with his nose buried in the daily with the red diamond logo.

Only one person in this building read '*Libé*' and that was the 'newcomer', Monsieur Djian, who *subscribed*. Monsieur Djian had moved into the second-floor flat ten months earlier. The brass plates beside the intercom had witnessed the arrival of a surname which stuck out among those of the families who had inhabited the building sometimes for several generations, most of which had an aristocratic ring to them. Monsieur Djian was in the import-export trade.

What did he import? What did he export? No one knew, but whatever it was it meant he could afford a Rolls-Royce, which – according to the concierge, who got it from Monsieur Djian himself – he had bought off 'his friend Jacques Séguéla', publicist to the stars.

His neighbours took this crowning glory of British automotive technology to be the height of vulgarity and openly referred to the Barritiers – the old Action Française family who had sold him their apartment in order to emigrate to the seventh *arrondissement* – as 'traitors'. They said hello to Monsieur Djian in passing, but it would never have occurred to them to ask him in.

When he first moved in, he had warmly invited them all to a drinks party at his new apartment, but each of his neighbours had managed to conjure up a prior arrangement they could not possibly get out of. Monsieur Djian did not hold it against them.

Though they saw him as an outsider, the occupants of the building had to admit Djian had one notable strong point: when it came to getting service charges knocked down, he was peerless. The management committee, who had until then never had any trouble getting their prim and proper residents to cough up, had had to get used to the idea of a city slicker calling the shots.

Undaunted, waving the estimates in front of them with his gold-Rolex-ringed wrist, Monsieur Djian would utter words like 'scandalous', 'crooks' and 'money-grabbers' to denote the various trades only too happy to ply their services around ageing Parisian apartment blocks: lift engineers, painters, plumbers and roofers.

He asked them to go back for revised quotes, threatened to sever long-standing business arrangements and demanded a reduction of at least twenty-five per cent. Monsieur Djian was physically rather imposing, and Madame Prusin of the Foncia property company was terrified into passing on all his requests.

The tradesmen, keen to avoid losing lucrative business, always replied favourably and in the most fawning terms. Monsieur Djian had thus saved the residents more than 38,000 francs so far this financial year. Not that they would have thanked him out loud; at meetings, they kept their mouths shut, sometimes gathering in small groups beforehand and agreeing in hushed tones: 'We'll let Djian take care of that ...'

Bernard was waiting for the lift – a Roux-Combaluzier 1911 model whose cab had recently been restored for thirty per cent less than originally quoted – when Monsieur Djian stepped out of it.

'Good morning, neighbour of mine!' Bernard greeted him brightly.

'Good morning,' Monsieur Djian replied, taken aback by such a sprightly welcome.

'I wanted to thank you on behalf of the residents' committee for the renovation of our lift.'

'I had no part in it,' objected Monsieur Djian.

'Oh but you did!' insisted Bernard, pointing his finger at him. 'It's thanks to you we got a fair quote, and not for the first time. You're a real asset to the running of this old building.'

Monsieur Djian mumbled a few words of thanks before his eyes fell on Bernard's '*Libé*'. He was holding his own copy in his hand. 'You read *Libération*, Monsieur Lavallière?'

'Absolutely. And I enjoy it, too. It's important to have a broad outlook. You really have to read *Le Figaro*, *Le Monde* and *Libération* to get any kind of understanding of what's going on in the world.'

'You're right,' agreed his neighbour, making way for Bernard to enter the lift.

'Now, you were kind enough to invite us round for drinks a few months ago but I was snowed under with work.'

'Aren't we all!' Monsieur Djian lamented.

'However, now I'd be delighted to take up your offer – I don't have much on at the moment. Just name your date.'

'How about Friday?' offered Monsieur Djian, caught on the hop.

'Perfect, Friday it is.'

Returning to his apartment, Bernard Lavallière hung up his hat and gabardine coat and, after scowling in the direction of the clock-painting, put his newspaper down on the breakfast table among the croissants. Charlotte choked on her Darjeeling; Bernard's two sons looked at him, mystified.

'What have you done with *Le Figaro*?' his wife asked anxiously.

'I didn't buy it,' he replied. 'It's good to have a change every now and then.'

His family stared as he sat down, poured himself coffee and unfolded what he had hitherto referred to as 'that leftie rag' – a fact his eldest son, Charles-Henri, did not pass up the opportunity to point out.

'Have you ever read it?' his father asked him, lowering the paper. Met with his first-born's silence, he declared that one ought to have some idea of what one is talking about before presuming to criticise. Then he added: 'We're going for drinks with the Djians on Friday.'

Coming out of a meeting on Avenue de l'Opéra, Bernard decided not to go back to the AXA offices. Everything he was working on could be be left until the morning. It was quarter to five and after waiting out a brief storm under the entrance to the building, he told himself a solitary stroll would do him the world of good.

His feet took him to the Palais-Royal and he found himself standing amid *Les Deux Plateaux*, more commonly known as Buren's Columns. The redevelopment of the courtyard outside the Ministry of Culture had caused quite a stir in the press. *Le Figaro* led the pack in its condemnation of what it saw as an attack on the city's historic monuments. The building of the columns had been the subject of several parliamentary debates and legal challenges, and had given rise to countless campaign groups and hundreds of petitions. Bernard had even signed one of them.

The flamboyant Culture Minister Jack Lang, all wry smiles and puffy hair, had been replaced by the rather more staid François Léotard. One of his first acts at the Ministry had been to look into halting the works, but he had soon given up on the idea – dismantling them would have ended up costing far more than completing them.

Opposed to the Buren columns on principle, Bernard had never actually seen them up close. The black and white pillars were reflected in pools of water, their varying heights creating a very attractive visual effect. So why had this work of art sparked such controversy?

He could remember clearly what the *cour d'honneur* had looked like before the work had started – it had been a car park, filled with nothing but row upon row of cars. And that was what everyone had made such a fuss about?

Children were playing on one of the lowest columns, jumping up and hopping down over and over again. Beyond them, a group of tourists stood over a metal grille, throwing coins onto the top of another column whose base, five metres down, was rooted in a strip of tarmac over which water flowed.

A Japanese woman's franc landed dead centre and she clapped her hands together before smiling at Bernard.

Passing through the archways of the Louvre, Bernard stopped dead in his tracks. The pyramid had sprung up from the ground. Though the Saint-Gobain glass panes were a long way off being fitted, the structure was there, and the stepped scaffolding around it made it look like one of the tombs at Saqqara.

Bernard took off his hat, the better to see it. This was modernity, right here in front of him, and it was all down to one man, the man whose name he had defended. The mammoth building works at the Grand Louvre had uncovered artefacts dating back to the Neolithic period and, from day one, the dig had given archaeologists the chance to unearth a lost Paris.

Who did they have to thank for it? Mitterrand, of course, and his ambitious '*grands travaux*' building programme including the Opéra Bastille, the Louvre Pyramid and the Grande Arche at La Défense, which Bernard turned to see was nearing completion.

François Mitterrand knew how to make his mark, earning his place in the history books as well as on the world stage. Sticking a glass pyramid in front of the Louvre, striped columns outside the Palais-Royal and a modern archway in line with the Arc de Triomphe smacked of an utterly anti-conservative, iconoclastic mentality – verging on the punk.

The hoarding surrounding the massive building site was covered in eye-catching graffiti, the work of several artists who had come together to produce a kind of long, esoteric fresco.

Bernard took a closer look at one of the designs, which looked more like a painting than a piece of graffiti: a pink hippopotamus with smaller hippos inside, blue ones this time. The big hippo was sticking out a kind of spiralling electric tongue; further on, the figure of a man with the head of a bird was holding a huge revolver, with a wide-eyed yellow cat perching on top.

These were powerful, unusual, bold works of art. What creativity! What imagination! Bernard said to himself as he followed the fresco all the way round the former Cour Napoléon.

If he spent an hour here, it would not be long enough to take in all of this long, inscrutable rebus of the modern world. He took a few steps back to look again at the enormous skeleton of the pyramid.

'Isn't it ghastly?'

Bernard turned to find a man with a grey goatee in a camel-hair coat standing beside him.

'As if we need a great big pyramid in front of the Louvre …' the man scoffed.

'Oh but we do,' replied Bernard, struggling to contain himself. 'We need a pyramid right here, and we need Buren's Columns too. We need it all and you and all the rest of them just don't get it, you haven't got a clue!'

'Oh I get it all right!' the man cawed. 'Look at you with your black hat and your scarf. I should have seen straight away you're one of them. Well, good for you!' And with that he turned on his heel.

Bernard watched him walk away. First, there had been the sly questions: 'You haven't gone leftie on us, have you, old chap?' This time, it was beyond doubt. The inhabitants of his world no longer recognised him as one of their own.

Sometimes life carries you in different directions and you don't even realise you've gone down a fork in the road; the great GPS of destiny has not followed the planned route and there has been no sign to indicate you've passed the point of no return. Life's Bermuda Triangle is both myth and reality.

One thing is certain: once you have come through this

kind of turbulence, you'll never return to the path you set out on. In the eyes of other people, he was on the Left. 'Hell is other people', that great man of the Left Sartre said, and he was right: hell was the de Vaunoys, Jean-Patrick Teraille and Colonel Larnier.

That bunch of narrow-minded parasites clinging to their convictions like mussels to their beds. The charge Bernard was leading against all the ideas he had once held, now toppling around him, was putting wind in his sails. How had Machiavelli put it? 'He must have a spirit that can change depending on the winds and variations of Fortune.'

As he walked briskly back under the archways of the Louvre, he could feel a profound change taking place within him. More than a change, a metamorphosis.

He placed one hand on his hat to keep it from flying off. The harder he held it down, the freer his mind seemed to be. It was as though he had travelled back in time, back to adolescence, when life stretches out before you and everything is still possible.

On his return to Rue de Passy, Charlotte announced that Monsieur Djian had called to cancel the drinks at his flat on Friday night. Disappointed, Bernard asked if Djian had had second thoughts.

'If only,' his wife replied. 'He's invited us to Jacques Séguéla's instead.'

Monsieur Djian had got his dates mixed up. Of course he wasn't free on Friday; that was the night Séguéla was throwing a huge party to celebrate the arrival of his portrait by Andy Warhol.

The painting had been held up at The Factory in New York since the artist's death earlier in the year. The publicist had just retrieved it and this was cause for celebration. The thought of putting off his neighbour, now that he had finally agreed to drinks, had been bothering Monsieur Djian for much of the afternoon when he had a brainwave: he could ask to bring his guests along. Séguéla would not turn him down.

This generous idea went on to spark what might be classed as a domestic incident two floors up.

'If you think I'm going to go sucking up to a roomful of leftie upstarts, you've got another thing coming,' Charlotte fumed. 'You go and have fun with your new friends without me.'

Charles-Henri, the eldest son, asked if he could go

instead, only to be reminded sharply by his mother that he had a society ball that evening.

Nobody brought it up again until the Friday. Under his wife's disapproving glare, Bernard put on his Prince of Wales suit jacket, slipped on his Burberry mac and donned his black felt hat.

'I'm off,' he said matter-of-factly.

Charlotte lowered her book and watched him leave without a word. Bernard walked down two flights of stairs and rang on the doorbell of the Djian residence.

'My wife is a little under the weather,' he announced.

The Rolls convertible sped along the avenues of Paris. Sitting in the back with her hair blowing in the wind and a far-off expression on her face, Madame Djian reminded him of those stunning, unobtainable Italian film stars of the 1960s. Monsieur Djian inserted a silver disc into the car radio. Digital audio. The strains of an electric guitar and synthetic harpsichord rang out inside the Rolls.

'This is a group called Images. They're friends of my daughter's, my eldest. It's at number one,' he said, chewing his cigar.

The Rolls swerved, jumping a red light, and Bernard began to laugh in surprise and amazement, as he had not done in decades – or perhaps ever before. 'They're taking me right through the night/ The demons of midnight,' sang the group whose name he had already forgotten, though every apartment block and even the starless sky of Paris rocked to their beat. Monsieur Djian bobbed his head in time to the music and it felt to Bernard as if the

Rolls had lifted up off the tarmac; even the headlights of passing cars seemed like little flickers of joy shining out from the darkness.

It was one of those nights that take you back to the magical nights of youth, filled with fun, freedom and boundary breaking – the kind of nights that naturally exist only in your imagination. The makers of this track were at the top of the charts, he was riding in a Rolls-Royce to meet the high priest of publicity and the man behind the wheel could knock any price down by thirty per cent. Winners, all of them.

As they drew closer to the party venue, the cars they passed began to change, as if the elegant town house had a magnetic field around it which made every vehicle in the neighbourhood morph into a Porsche Carrera, Rolls Silver Spur or Lamborghini.

Two men on the door politely asked to see their invitations, crossed their names off the list and opened the gate. In the marble hallway, they handed their coats to some girls with incredible legs and followed the music: rock, or maybe it was pop, the words spoken off-beat in German with a chorus that went 'Rock me Amadeus', as far as Bernard could tell.

Inside the vast reception room, there must have been at least three hundred people engaged in loud conversation, each holding a glass of champagne. Two saxophonists in black glasses and white silk suits were standing on gold cubes riffing on the song, while a disco ball the size of a planet rotated above them. Waiters wearing red shell suits of the kind worn by garage attendants handed round trays of canapés.

'I'll introduce you,' said Monsieur Djian as they entered the fray.

The girls, who had blue streaks in their mane-like hair and mostly wore a single earring, were swaying from side to side like seaweed. Many of the men had their hair tied back in ponytails and some sported the anti-racism yellow hand symbol on their jackets.

Suddenly Jacques Séguéla appeared before them. He was with the sculptor César, who looked even smaller in real life and had such a bouncy beard he must put rollers in it.

Séguéla was wearing a purple jacket over a thin black polo neck. Standing behind César with both hands placed on his shoulders, he was midway through the story of how the sculptor had compressed his collection of branded food tins and turned it into art, when he turned to Djian.

'You made it,' he said with a smile that puffed out his tanned cheeks, 'and here's the fairest of them all,' he added, leaning in to plant a lingering kiss on Madame Djian's neck.

'Monsieur Lavallière,' said Djian.

'Welcome!' replied the man behind the Citroën ads. 'You don't have a drink ... Champagne!' he cried, and one of the red garage attendants came running.

'I'll be right back. Look after my wife for me,' said Djian, but she had already drifted off to join another group.

This is where it's all happening, Bernard said to himself, and I'm right here, in the heart of it. A splash of champagne spattered his blazer.

'Sorry,' said Bernard Tapie, brushing his shoulder. 'It won't stain. Cheers!' he added, smiling broadly.

Bernard clinked glasses with this other Bernard who had had stints as a racing driver, singer, businessman, manager of a cycling team, manager of a football club and TV presenter, and was set to try his hand at politics next. Lavallière could not have felt more out of place – it was as though he had been teleported in from another era – but he pushed further into the thick of it, having given up all hope of finding Djian.

'Pretty cool to have your portrait painted by Warhol, eh?' The man, who wore a black T-shirt under his suit and held a cigarette in his fingertips, looked familiar – he had probably seen him on TV – but Bernard could not for the life of him put a name to the face. He had a schoolboy haircut and a strange, fixed smile.

'Yes, it's a great privilege,' Bernard replied soberly.

'That's exactly what it is, a great privilege,' the man replied. 'I'll remember that.' He walked away.

'You know, it's a great privilege to have your portrait painted by Warhol,' he regurgitated immediately to a fellow wearing his white hair in a ponytail, who nodded in agreement.

The Warhol was mounted on a velvet-covered pedestal and was protected by a layer of bulletproof glass. The publicist's face appeared four times in the picture, highlighted in orange and white. Red and lilac geometric patterns were layered up to create a rather pleasing prism effect.

'Not another Warhol fanatic, are you?'

Bernard turned to face a slender man with a salt-and-pepper beard so short it was like sandpaper. 'I don't know,' he replied, taking another look at the painting. 'Warhol's had his day really, hasn't he?' he declared, trying to sound as if he knew what he was talking about.

The man seemed interested by this, so Bernard went on to tell him about his discovery of Buren's Columns, the pyramid at the Louvre and the graffiti on the hoardings, all those new shapes, that hippopotamus. He surprised himself by frequently using the word 'radical'.

'I intend to carry out some *grands travaux* of my own,' he concluded as he polished off his third glass of champagne.

'Basquiat's your man,' the man with the stubble pronounced with great solemnity. 'Do you know the work of Jean-Michel Basquiat?'

Bernard shook his head.

'It's still affordable. Here's the number for my gallery.'

'Not going on about Basquiat again, are you?' They were interrupted by a man, then swiftly joined by another who was swilling his wine with an air of irony.

'Don't take any notice of them; they're museum types.'

The conversation was lively, from what Bernard understood of it. An exhibition entitled 'The Era, the Fashion, the Morals, the Passion' was due to open at the Pompidou Centre, highlighting the international art movements of the 1980s, yet no one had thought to include the works of this Basquiat chap.

'Shame on you!' said the man with the sandpaper beard.

Leaving the three of them to squabble over this mysterious painter, Bernard picked up another glass of champagne and turned his mind back to his ancestor. Charles-Édouard was a shrewd character, no doubt about it, but in common with many of his peers, the Impressionists had completely passed him by. A single Monet, a single Renoir – not to mention a Gauguin or a Van Gogh – would now be worth a hundred times the legacy he had built up over his lifetime. The Lavallières had displayed a dubious penchant for paintings of ruins – as far as romantic landscapes went, they had it covered – but had never had the sense to invest in anything of artistic worth. A repulsive image came into his mind: the little landscape painting with its broken clock.

'Very well, I want a Basquiat,' he said, downing his champagne.

No one reacted.

'Did you hear me? I want to buy a Basquiat, right now, this minute.'

'You're going to spend 150,000 francs on a Basquiat?' asked the man from the museum.

'Yes, that's exactly what I'm going to do,' replied Bernard.

The man with the sandpaper beard asked him to wait quarter of an hour while he fetched his car.

A tray of salmon canapés went past. He took one just as the speakers began pumping out a tune chanted by a woman begging someone called Andy to say yes. One hundred and fifty thousand francs wasn't exactly small change, but he was past caring. If worst came to worst, he could always sell one of the smaller flats he had inherited, which would bring in a darn sight more than 150,000 francs – enough to buy several Basquiats. Damn, it felt good to live in the eighties and really make the most of it; he had not felt so alive in years.

Monsieur Djian reappeared, offering his apologies for having had to say hello to so many people.

'I hope you're not bored?' he said.

'Not at all. I'm going to buy a painting.'

'Good for you,' he replied approvingly, before walking away again.

Close by, Jack Lang was deep in conversation with a blonde woman smoking a gold-tipped Sobranie cigarette. She had to be an actress or a singer but, once again, Bernard failed to place her.

When she walked away, Bernard took the opportunity to approach Lang on the subject of Buren's Columns. He told him he had seen children playing and tourists throwing coins on them – music to the ears of the former minister.

He looked Bernard in the eye. 'Governments come and go. Life is the only movement that keeps going,' he said with a solemn, knowing smile. He placed his hand on Bernard's forearm and went on. 'It's all part of a great burst of creativity, a real exploration of the age we live in. You should join my movement, Allons z'Idées,' he said, taking a sticker out of his pocket bearing a Warhol-style picture of himself.

The minister was pulled away, there was movement among the guests and Bernard found himself once again standing next to Jacques Séguéla, who was saying: 'Money doesn't have ideas; only ideas can make money … and it's our job to have ideas.'

Making his way towards the exit, he brushed past Serge July, founder of *Libération*, who was informing a shaven-headed man that it was now impossible to tell where culture began and advertising finished. Bernard gathered his belongings, put on his Burberry trench coat and placed his hat on his head. He smoothed down the brim and ducked into the crowd one last time to say goodbye to his host.

'An image is worth a thousand words, as Mao Zedong said,' Jacques Séguéla was now telling a group of young people hanging on his every word, when his eye fell on Bernard. The man who traded on his flashes of genius then had one which passed over his own head.

'It's Mitterrand's hat!' he exclaimed, pointing to the Homburg.

And how they all laughed at the joke from the man behind Mitterrand's slogan: '*La force tranquille*'.

The gallery owner switched on the strip lights which flickered for a while before settling down. Bernard had kept his hat on. He stood with his hands in his pockets, waiting for the owner to get 'the Basquiats' out for him.

'Why isn't he in the major galleries?' asked Bernard.

'Because he's young and black,' replied the owner.

Black, as well, mused Bernard.

'That's him over there,' he added, pointing to a small photo hanging on the wall.

Bernard saw the face of a young witch doctor with intense eyes and spiky hair.

'Jean-Michel's a French name.'

'That's right, from Haiti, where Basquiat's family come from.'

'Does he speak French?'

'When he feels like it,' quipped the gallery owner.

Then he produced three canvases, turned so that Bernard could only see their frames.

'Close your eyes and prepare to see the work of a budding genius.'

The three paintings had echoes of the artwork on the hoardings at the Louvre, yet they carried a force that was at once tribal and urban, unlike anything he had encountered before.

Having been brought up on eighteenth-century landscapes, Bernard was completely unprepared for the impact they had on him. The power radiating off these pictures was almost radioactive. The paint strokes, the figures, the little planes and crossed-out phrases exploded out of the canvas like a jumbled message from a lost civilisation to be uncovered five thousand years down the line; *our* lost civilisation.

Within their frames, they held the story of humanity's primal rituals. The feast-day incantations and mystical elegies of man's beginnings were fused with the noise of aeroplanes and the sirens of police cars. Blackened figures stared mask-like at the viewer, while childlike planes flew across the sky, colliding with words scattered over the canvas like a crazy game of Scrabble.

Bernard stood in silence for several minutes, unable to take his eyes off the paintings, like a mouse transfixed at the sight of a snake.

There was no going back. Tonight, a new Bernard Lavallière was coming to life between the cold, damp concrete walls of a modern art gallery. Whilst his friends and family would no doubt recoil from Jean-Michel

Basquiat's works like a vampire from sunlight, putting *that* on his living-room wall would be a defining act. The mark of a man in the know, with his finger on the pulse.

'What are they called?' he asked softly.

The salesman introduced them from left to right: '*Sangre Corpus*, *Wax wing* and *Radium*.'

'I'd like thirty per cent off if I take all three.'

'Fifteen …' replied the dealer.

The following week, Bernard began his *grands travaux*, literally and figuratively. The radical change in his outlook coincided with the arrival of a team of painters.

His wife looked on in horror as the cornicing was ripped off and the fabric on the walls torn down to make way for a coat of perfectly white paint. Valuers from the Salle Drouot auction house came for the family furniture and Bernard watched it go without an ounce of regret. Not for the Louis XVI dresser and two Ming vases, or the gilt bronze carriage clock with Diana the huntress and a fawn; not for the Louis XIII cabinet, the six matching Louis XVI armchairs, the Louis-Philippe stool or the desk of the same era.

The eighteenth-century landscapes of ruins filed past, followed by the pastel drawing of the woman gazing upwards, the Aubusson tapestry and even the Charles X crystal chandelier.

With undisguised joy, he had given instructions for the clock-picture to be sold without a reserve. Charlotte Lavallière, née Charlotte de Gramont, removed all her family heirlooms to the safety of her boudoir. Everything else went to the auctioneers.

Only the portrait of Charles-Édouard Lavallière survived this organised apocalypse and it was under his gaze, fixed in oil paint in 1883, that the Jean-Michel Basquiat canvases arrived one morning.

Charlotte threatened to divorce him, but she did not go through with it. Bernard agreed to a compromise: one Basquiat in the living room, the other two in his office at AXA. They were the first in a long line of acquisitions, and Bernard sold a studio flat inherited from his ancestor to fund his newfound passion for art.

'Supposing the Left get in again in '88,' the voices of the business world began to whisper. 'Bernard would be a precious asset.'

'Lavallière's a socialist?' asked some.

'Of course,' replied others, 'he's always been a Mitterrand man.'

Bernard's meteoric rise in the art-collecting world had given his career a boost too. At AXA, he was soon considered cutting edge. He was often photographed at private views for the society pages of *Vogue* or *Elle*, which his secretary excitedly passed around the office.

He was sometimes seen, champagne in hand, at the side of Jack Lang or the actor Pierre Arditi. He got on well with Claude Berri too – though the two men never saw eye to eye on Robert Ryman's white monochrome paintings.

The famous filmmaker even took him round to Serge Gainsbourg's house one afternoon where, against all expectations, Bernard came up against a rather rigid character as far as painting was concerned, who lectured him on Cranach's nudes which he ranked above all else in the history of art.

One morning, as he went to buy his copy of '*Libé*', one of those sudden, unexpected, absurd and totally out-of-the-ordinary events happened, the kind journalists with little knowledge of the basic principles of André Breton's movement like to describe as 'surreal': Bernard had his hat stolen.

It was all over in a matter of seconds; it happened so quickly he did not even have the presence of mind to cry out, still less run after his assailant. He was left standing on the pavement, dumbfounded and slightly dishevelled.

Daniel Mercier felt as if he had the combined power of the French rugby team. He had never run so fast, for so long, through the streets of Paris, or any other city, for that matter. He stopped and leant against a heavy carriage door to catch his breath. To look at the hat, too, and check the presidential initials on the inside. Everything was fine. It was the right hat, and he had got it back. Even if his efforts to trace it had occupied every waking hour for several months.

After reading Pierre Aslan's last letter he had been able to piece together what had happened on the evening the perfumer had lost the hat at the brasserie. A man with the initials B.L. had left with Mitterrand's hat. Daniel had the address of the brasserie and the date of the dinner.

There was just one thing missing: the brasserie's list of reservations for that evening. Customers who telephone to book a table have to leave their names. The relevant page in the restaurant's diary might hold the key to the identity of the mysterious B.L. Daniel had confided his conclusions to his wife.

'That hat will drive you insane if you're not careful,' she had warned.

'I can't give up now. I have to follow up any lead that might help me find the hat,' he had retorted.

So one Saturday morning, Daniel had driven to Paris and headed for the address given him by Aslan. When he got there, it struck him that all brasseries look the same with their big red awnings, the oyster bar outside and waiters in white aprons. The maître d' had opened a big, rectangular book bound in claret leather.

'Daniel Mercier ... Ah yes, table 15. Waiter! Please take Monsieur to his table.'

The maître d' who held the object Daniel desperately wanted to consult was grey-haired and about fifty. He didn't look as if he would be easy to coax information from, still less like he would be open to bribery.

On the motorway coming to Paris, Daniel had run through all the ways he might be able to consult the restaurant's diary, from the simplest – looking through it discreetly when the maître d' left it next to the cash register – to the riskiest: snatching it out of his hands and making off with it as fast as his legs could carry him.

Daniel had mused on the possible outcome of the latter solution, imagining himself being pursued by a pack of brasserie waiters, like the speeded-up chase scenes at the end of each episode of *The Benny Hill Show*.

He had also considered bribing the maître d' and had withdrawn a 500-franc note from the bank to that end. But judging by the look of the man now greeting a couple of English diners, he would never take the bait. The claret leather book passed in front of Daniel's table several times, as though taunting him: Look, I'm right here with the head waiter and you'll never get your hands on me.

To calm his nerves, Daniel ordered a dozen oysters, a bottle of Pouilly-Fuissé and a plate of salmon with dill. He drank his first glass down in one. The chilled wine eased his anxiety. He would find a solution.

What that was, he had no idea, but he would not leave this place without the information he needed. As the spoonful of shallot vinegar spread over the surface of a slightly milky oyster, Daniel held his breath. He worked the mollusc free with the small, flat fork, lifted it to his mouth and closed his eyes.

No sooner had the combination of marine saltiness and vinegar touched his tongue than the President's words rang out once more, as clear as when he had heard them for the very first time: 'As I was saying to Helmut Kohl last week ...' Since his dinner *en compagnie* with the head of state, the same thing had happened each time he ate vinegared oysters.

Daniel swallowed his last oyster and looked towards the bar. Customers not eating lunch were drinking coffee, or kirs, or glasses of Sauvignon, reading the capital's daily paper, *Le Parisien*. Some were obviously regulars.

The young barman, a blond chap with very short hair who looked no older than twenty-two or twenty-three, shook their hand when they arrived or left. When he wasn't putting fresh glasses of white wine in front of the regulars, he was busy preparing coffees for the dining room at large and filling pitchers of water or carafes of wine.

He must be a beginner in the business, thought Daniel, probably not that well paid, since he wouldn't share in the tips left for waiters serving at the tables. He's the one, thought Daniel, fixing his gaze on the young man. He'll take my 500 francs. He will be my Trojan Horse, my way into the claret leather book.

Daniel paid for his lunch, left a ten-franc tip in the chrome dish on the table, got to his feet, took a deep breath and headed for the bar, where only two customers were left, one finishing a kir, the other a glass of beer. Daniel perched on a stool and made a show of opening *Le Parisien*.

'What can I get you, Monsieur?' asked the young barman.

'Coffee, please.'

Daniel made his espresso last while he waited for the two men at the bar to clear off, hoping that others would not take their place. The one with the beer drank up and left without a word, closely followed by the kir drinker, who shook the barman's hand. *Voilà*, Daniel was alone.

'I'll have another coffee,' he said to the barman.

Deftly, the young man detached the filter holder from the machine, scooped in a portion of ground coffee and replaced it, pulling the handle sideways to pack it tight. Daniel slipped his hand inside his jacket and and took out his wallet.

'How much do I owe you?'

'Two coffees, eight francs, Monsieur.'

Daniel fished out the right money in coins, subtly taking out the 500-franc note at the same time. The young man placed the coffee on the bar in front of Daniel and collected the cash. Daniel chose his moment and unfolded the note on the marble counter. The barman glanced at the note, then looked at Daniel, who fixed him with a penetrating stare.

'There's something else you can do for me,' he said, in tones as intense as his expression.

'Really, I don't think so,' replied the young man, heading back to the coffee machine.

'Five coffees on twelve!' called a waiter.

The barman set out the cups, then walked back to where Daniel was sitting, and leant across the bar.

'Listen, I'm not a poof, OK?' he said, in a low voice.

Daniel had anticipated everything but this. Horrified that his approach had been mistaken for an attempted pick-up, he struggled to find a way to retrieve the situation as rapidly as possible. An idea – truly a stroke of genius, he was to reflect later – crossed his mind.

'Me neither,' he heard himself reply. 'I'm a private detective.'

The young man turned to look at him. A surprised, intrigued smile lit his features. Daniel knew he had won. The barman's head would be full of images from films and TV series, he thought. And clearly, it was. The barman abandoned his row of coffee cups.

'Are you serious?'

'Deadly serious,' said Daniel. 'It's about the restaurant bookings diary. Help me and the note's all yours.'

'Go on,' said the barman, moving nearer.

'Where are my five coffees?' called the waiter.

Unconsciously, Daniel had taken inspiration from his favourite fictional detective, Parisian gumshoe Nestor Burma and from *Mike Hammer* on Canal +. Véronique never missed an episode. Whenever he told someone that he was a private detective, Hammer, played by Stacy Keach, always got their full attention.

And as it turned out it worked like a charm in real life, too. What's more the fictional Frenchman and the American tough guy both sported Homburgs, which Daniel took as an excellent omen.

'I'll see what I can do; come back at seven,' said Sébastien – his name was printed on his silver-plated identity bracelet.

Getting further into character, Daniel tore the note in two, saying that he would be back that evening with the other half.

He spent the afternoon wandering aimlessly around Paris, even visiting Parc Monceau where Mademoiselle Marquant said she had left the hat on a bench. Daniel sat down on a similar bench and thought back over the short story that had won the Prix Balbec. Here was the sequel, though Fanny would never know it.

At seven o'clock sharp, he pushed open the door of the brasserie and headed for the bar. Three men were sipping drinks, while Sébastien wiped glasses. Daniel and Sébastien glanced at one another.

'Coffee,' said Daniel.

The young man slung his tea towel over his shoulder, grasped the handle of the filter holder, scooped in a portion of coffee and screwed it into the machine. The steam whistled. He reached up to a shelf above the bar, took down a copy of *Le Parisien*, and walked over to Daniel.

'Page 21,' he muttered before turning back to his sink full of glasses.

Daniel opened the newspaper and held his breath. Page 12, page 18, page 21 ... a photocopy of the relevant page from the restaurant diary had been slipped inside the newspaper. He had done it.

His eyes ran down the list of names. Which of them could be B.L.? The first name written by the maître d'hôtel, at the top of the list, was 'Aslan', a table for three. Other names followed, none of them beginning with the right letter. What if B.L. had not booked, just as he, Daniel, had not booked on that famous evening when he had sat next to the President?

The trail would go cold right here, for ever. It would be over.

Happily, though, between Jacques Franquier, two people, and Robineau, five people, there was a surname beginning with 'L', but no first name: Lavallière, four people.

Daniel folded the sheet of paper and slipped it into his pocket. Checking that no one was looking, he took out the second half of the 500-franc note and quickly shut it inside the newspaper.

Sébastien brought him his coffee.

'Page 21,' said Daniel in an offhand way. 'Good work, kid,' he added, because that seemed exactly the sort of thing a real private detective would say.

Back at home, Daniel dialled 12 for directory enquiries and found only three Lavallières listed in the Paris phone book: a Xavier Lavallière in the eighth *arrondissement*, an Hélène in the seventh, and a Jean in the greater Paris region. There were others, but they were ex-directory.

Shut away in his study, he stood at the window, looking out over the city of Rouen with the same brooding air as J. R. Ewing gazing out over Dallas from his high-rise office at Ewing Oil whenever things weren't going his way.

Unlike J.R., he had no minibar to pour himself a drink from. J.R. almost always had his best ideas at the end of an episode, sipping a whisky on the rocks. His face would light up with a sardonic smile, the image would freeze and the words 'Executive Producer Philip Capice' would flash up on the screen in large yellow letters.

Daniel sat back in his armchair and sighed. The TV was still on, with the sound turned down, and that bouffant-haired scoundrel Jean-Luc Lahaye was mouthing his love for the whole of womankind. What Daniel grandly referred to as his 'study' was also the family TV room, where they enjoyed supper on a tray every week in front of the Saturday-night variety show *Champs-Élysées*.

Daniel picked up the remote and turned the television off. Just as he was thinking he had considered every possible way of tracking down the elusive Lavallière whose first name must begin with 'B', suddenly the glimmer of an idea sparked in his mind. An embryonic plan, like a tiny glow-worm in the night.

He took the perfumer's letter out of his folder. 'A hat that was identical to yours in every particular,' Pierre Aslan had written. The same make, thought Daniel, just as his son came into the study, a glass of grenadine cordial in his hand, announcing that it was time for *Knight Rider*.

'Yes, yes, in a second, *mon chéri*,' muttered Daniel, tapping the name of the hatter from memory into his Minitel keyboard. The address and telephone number appeared on the screen.

'Yes, good afternoon,' said Daniel, airily. 'It's one of your clients here, Monsieur Lavallière – just making sure you have my new address for your files.'

'I'm afraid I don't know, Monsieur,' replied a young woman's voice. 'I'll get the file, if you'd like to hold for a second.'

An interminable minute, or two, went by, during which Daniel had time to loosen his tie and drink almost the whole glass of grenadine left on the desk by Jérôme.

The young woman picked up the receiver again. 'Hello? Let me see, Monsieur Lavallière ... Bernard Lavallière?' she asked.

Daniel thought he would faint.

'Yes,' he managed to say, 'now, what address do you have?'

'Number 16, Rue de Passy in the sixteenth, Monsieur.'

Daniel banged down the receiver and took a deep breath.

'I've got it,' he murmured to himself. 'I've got it ...' and he sank back into his armchair, as if struck by a knock-out blow.

'It's starting!' yelled Jérôme, settling himself on the rug about a metre from the TV screen.

Daniel turned up the volume. In a strange purple desert, David Hasselhoff's Pontiac Firebird roared towards the spectator from out of the middle distance. Against the catchy, synthesised-drum theme tune, the opening voice-over promised 'A shadowy flight into the dangerous world of a man who does not exist. Michael Knight, a young loner on a crusade to champion the cause of the innocent, the helpless, the powerless, in a world of criminals who operate above the law.'

The sequence was intercut with shots of the black car flying through the air in a series of unlikely stunts. The theme tune became hypnotic and Jérôme began bobbing his head to the beat.

Galvanised by the music and the exploits of K.I.T.T., the car's futuristic onboard computer, Daniel found himself nodding along, too. Nothing would stand in the way of the lone knight now, he was certain of that.

The following weekend, the lone knight set out once more for the capital, not at the wheel of a daredevil Pontiac Firebird, but a modest Audi 5000 family saloon. Staking out no. 16, Rue de Passy, he saw a man in a dark coat and a black hat leave the building. Daniel followed him to the newspaper kiosk.

The man bought a copy of *Libération*. Waiting for the

lights to change, they were just centimetres apart. Daniel stared, eyes wide, at the black felt hat.

It was his, he would stake his life on it. He recognised the slight signs of wear around the dent in the crown; he knew every detail of that hat by heart.

He should have reached out, snatched the hat and run off with it, but he found himself incapable of such daring. His legs felt like lead and when he tried to lift his hand, it began to tremble.

He was so overcome that he could not even step out onto the pedestrian crossing when Bernard Lavallière did so. Welded to the pavement, Daniel had watched him walk all the way back to no. 16, Rue de Passy.

But now, he had conquered his fear. He had done it. He had got Mitterrand's hat back. Leaning with his back against the carriage doorway, gasping for breath, he placed the black felt hat on his head and closed his eyes.

He had triumphed over every obstacle like a fairy-tale hero crossing kingdoms, rivers, forests and mountains in search of the golden apple or the magic stone that would bring them power and glory, or simply the satisfaction of a challenge met.

His hand trailed over the water. He touched the surface with his finger, drawing a line across the still, green expanse of the Adriatic. The black hull passed silently under one of the city's 420 bridges, plunging Daniel, Véronique and Jérôme briefly into shadow, before the sun reappeared.

Daniel had dreamt up the idea of a return trip to Venice, twelve years after their honeymoon, during his quest for the hat. If I find it, he had told himself, we'll go to Venice. It would mark the end of the search.

He had decided to stay at the same hotel, with its terrace overlooking the Dogana but this time with Jérôme, who had been fascinated by the prisons at the Doge's Palace with their iron bars as thick as your arm.

This was the second gondola ride they had taken since they'd arrived – gondolas were far too expensive to be used as everyday transport.

Daniel was the first to step ashore, wearing his hat. He held out a hand to Véronique as his son jumped straight onto the quay. It was time for a coffee break at Caffè Florian, in Piazza San Marco. The three of them made their way down Calle Vallaresso, passing under the arches of the Museo Correr, where Véronique had insisted, yesterday, on returning to see Carpaccio's celebrated *Two Venetian Ladies*.

It had been an opportunity to explain to Jérôme that, yes, the name of the raw beef dish that Papa often ordered at the pizzeria was also the name of a famous painter. Jérôme had asked whether the painter liked raw beef so much the dish had been named after him.

'Absolutely,' said his father. 'Carpaccio was well known at his local pizzeria.'

It was not their first visit of the day to Piazza San Marco. In Venice, all roads lead to that beating heart of the city on the lagoon. Each time it was like a dream, bustling with little figures, pigeons, shadows and sun.

As they headed for Caffè Florian, Véronique elbowed her husband. 'Daniel …' she said, breathlessly, 'look who's there.'

François Mitterrand was crossing the square with a woman, who was followed by a little girl with very long brown hair. He was wearing his usual coat and a red scarf, but no hat. Pigeons scattered into the air as they approached.

Daniel was not the only tourist rooted to the spot by the President's sudden appearance. A man smiled at the head of state, who responded with a brief nod. Then he stepped out of the sunlight and walked away beneath the arches of the Procuratie.

'He's here,' said Véronique, quietly. 'At the same time as us.'

Daniel put a hand up to the Homburg and gently smoothed the brim. The hat and the President had just passed within metres of each other. It was a disturbing thought, and Daniel was still troubled by it as they sat sipping Cokes on the terrace of Caffè Florian.

It was absurd. Of course François Mitterrand had the means to buy himself another black hat. He had almost certainly done just that, and in fact probably had several hats – perhaps he had even lost hats before or thrown some away because they were worn out. Still, it was as if something was missing from the figure that represented France all over the world.

By depriving the President of his hat, had Daniel not committed an ultimately very selfish and sacrilegious act, like those tourists who insist on taking away tiny fragments of the Temple of Luxor, or the Acropolis, with the risible idea of displaying them on their mantelpiece? They were making off with sacred relics to which they had no right, and which – most importantly – did not belong to them.

For the first time, Daniel felt guilty and uncomfortable, like someone who has just broken a treasured possession.

That afternoon, they visited the Bovolo. The name, meaning 'snail', referred to the external staircase of the Palazzo Contarini. The Renaissance masterpiece featured a six-storey spiral staircase enclosed in a tower circled by a corresponding spiral of multiple arches and delicate white columns.

From the top, there was a fine view over the rooftops of Venice, and a gentle breeze on your face.

'Remember?' said Daniel, as they began the short climb. 'The little horse …' Véronique smiled.

Twelve years earlier, they had climbed the Bovolo after visiting Murano, where a glass-blower had made a little horse for them as they watched and presented it to them as a souvenir.

That afternoon, Daniel had hidden it at the top of the Bovolo. The staircase was covered by a round roof of wooden beams, which you could reach if you stood on tiptoe.

Sliding his hand along one of the beams, his fingers had encountered a coin, then another, a key-ring, a souvenir brooch, then more coins, from all over the world. Lovers, and lovers of Venice, had dug into their pockets and left a token of their passing. Daniel had taken out the little glass horse and slipped it onto one of the beams.

Two young German girls were taking photographs of each other in front of the Venetian roofs, and a man was filming a panoramic 180-degree shot with a large VHS camera.

Véronique told Jérôme to be careful near the edge, while Daniel looked up at the beams overhead. He removed his hat, placed it on the stone balustrade and lifted his hand. He thought he remembered leaving the little horse in the left-hand corner. He felt a coin, a piece of cardboard – perhaps a plane ticket – another coin.

'You won't find it,' said Véronique, just as his fingers touched something smooth and cold.

He removed the small object from the wooden beam as if he were picking a fruit.

'Look,' he said, amazed.

Daniel was holding the little horse in his hand. Jérôme came and stood beside his father, who looked at Véronique, whose eyes were misted with tears.

She was overcome with emotion at the thought that the little horse had been waiting for them in its hiding place for twelve years. Daniel handed the horse to Jérôme and took his wife in his arms.

A gust of wind blew her hair across his face and he closed his eyes. When he opened them again, the black hat had disappeared from the stone balustrade.

The nightmare was beginning all over again.

'This can't be happening. It can't be ...' muttered Daniel, as he raced down the stairs, his heart beating wildly. The Bovolo's shallow steps seemed endless, like a sequence in a dream, where time and gravity are suspended.

The hat wasn't in the street below, nor in the garden at the bottom of the staircase. Perhaps it had skimmed over the rooftops, and the wind had blown it down one of the adjacent alleyways?

Daniel ran towards one of them. But there was no sign of the hat there either. Tears of rage and anguish welled up in his eyes. He felt he could sit down in the street, right there, and howl. Then he spotted an elderly man with a walking stick, flanked by two women – doubtless his wife and daughter.

The man was holding a black hat in his hand. On his own head, he sported an elegant cream felt hat with a crimson band. Daniel raced towards him.

'It's mine! That's my hat!' he said breathlessly.

'*È francese*,' said the man, smiling. 'Don't worry, Monsieur,' he said in French, with a strong Italian accent. 'I found your little note inside. I do the same myself,' he added, with another friendly smile. And the old man held the hat out to Daniel.

'Thank you, sir. Thank you very much,' said Daniel, clutching the hat.

'Good day to you,' said the old man. And he lifted his own hat in a gesture of farewell before turning and walking away, resuming his conversation with the two women in Italian.

Daniel stared at his hat and turned it upside down. He saw the white silk lining the crown, and the leather band with the initials.

He felt underneath the band with two fingers. When he had felt a little way round, his fingers touched something and his heart gave a lurch. He took out a small piece of paper folded in four and opened it. 'Reward: with thanks.' And a telephone number.

The slip of paper had been there all along. The hat had contained its own SOS message since the beginning. None of the people who had worn it subsequently had thought to look inside and see if the owner had left a message. Only a true hat connoisseur would know that trick.

The handwriting was familiar – it had been seen all over France during the election campaign, in the form of the signature on pamphlets.

It was François Mitterrand's handwriting.

'It's your decision,' said Véronique after dinner.

He let his wife and son go on ahead to the hotel room, saying he needed time to think.

'I'm going to take a stroll,' he announced.

Now he was alone in a narrow, dimly lit street. The slap of the water echoed against the ancient stones. With the hat on his head and his hands behind his back, he had climbed to the top of the steeply arched bridge and gazed at the moonlight reflected in the canal.

Under the black hat, the latest developments swirled about in his brain; Daniel tried to make sense of it all.

He was here in Venice at the same time as the hat's legitimate owner, and he had just found the message tucked behind the leather band. Perhaps the elderly Italian who had returned the hat to him was just one element of an overall scheme – even the gust of wind that had blown the hat away seemed to be part of a scenario whose pieces were falling into place.

It seemed to him quite clear that an appeal had been

made to him, Daniel Mercier of SOGETEC, who, without this hat, would still be in Paris taking orders from Jean Maltard. Because Mitterrand's hat had changed the course of his life, there was no denying that.

Mademoiselle Marquant, too, had seen her destiny altered, and that strange fellow, Aslan, had created a new fragrance. What had Bernard Lavallière done? He didn't know, but perhaps the hat had changed his life, too.

The presidential election was approaching, Daniel reminded himself, and the President was placing himself – and the nation – in the hands of fate. A *motoscafo* passed slowly under the bridge. Its lights projected a huge, looming shadow onto the faded plaster façades of the buildings lining the canal. A man in a coat and hat.

Daniel stepped back in alarm. He knew the shadow was his, but what he saw was the silhouette of François Mitterrand, immense and majestic, facing him for a few brief seconds before the darkness engulfed it.

That was the deciding sign. He knew now what he must do.

Back in the hotel room, Daniel declared solemnly, 'I will call the number tomorrow.' Then he undressed.

The last thing he removed was the hat. He placed it on a side table near the window, in a shaft of moonlight.

'Is there a number we can call you back on, Monsieur?'

Daniel gave the room number, then hung up. That was it. No going back.

'*Secrétaire générale*, Élysée Palace,' the voice had said, answering his call. Daniel had explained the story of the hat and the young woman had asked him to wait for a moment.

The room telephone rang fifteen minutes later. A man addressed Daniel, very politely.

'We must ask you to be discreet, Monsieur Mercier: I suppose you have seen the initials inside the hat …?'

'Yes, I have.'

'Then I suppose you understand whose hat it is?'

'Yes.'

'And so I can count on your discretion …'

'You can indeed,' said Daniel, 'though I do have one request.'

'Yes?' said the man at the other end of the line.

'I should like to hand the hat back to the owner myself.'

'That is precisely how the owner of the hat would like to receive it, Monsieur Mercier. He suggests meeting at Caffè Florian at five o'clock, in the first room on the left as you come in.'

At 4.40 p.m., Daniel put Mitterrand's hat on one last time, kissed Véronique and Jérôme, and left them on the steps of Santa Maria della Salute.

'I have an appointment with François Mitterrand, I'll be back shortly,' he announced loudly, in front of a group of tourists who turned round to stare.

Then he walked off in the direction of a gondola. He didn't quibble over the fare for the ride to San Marco, nor did he sit on the little red leather seat, but remained standing in the middle of the boat with the hat on his head and his face caressed by the warm salt air of the Adriatic.

At the entrance to Caffè Florian, he was approached by the Brylcreemed Italian head waiter, a rotund man with a slender moustache.

'I have a meeting with François Mitterrand,' said Daniel, taking off his hat.

The maître d' inclined his head and led the way silently to the small room off to the left. Beneath a fresco of an angel, the President of the French Republic was sitting at a small white marble table. He was wearing a dark coat and a claret-coloured scarf. He got to his feet.

'*Bonjour, Monsieur Mercier.*' He shook Daniel's hand.

'*Bonjour, Monsieur le Président*,' answered Daniel.

Then, at the President's invitation, he sat down next to him. François Mitterrand ordered a coffee, which was brought immediately on a silver tray.

'There is a reward, as indicated on the slip of paper,' announced the First Frenchman.

'No,' said Daniel, quietly, 'I don't want a reward.'

François Mitterrand gave a partly amused, partly resigned smile.

'Since you do not want a reward, I will tell you a secret … This hat … I did not lose it in Venice, but in Paris, some time ago.' He paused. 'It must have had quite a few adventures before ending up on this table,' he added, stroking the felt, 'but we shall never know.' He stared at Daniel, smiling enigmatically.

'No, we'll never know,' said Daniel, transfixed by the President's gaze.

There was a further silence, and then François Mitterrand bent forward to take small sips of his coffee. Through the half-open window, Daniel glimpsed the sunlit Piazza San Marco and the crowds passing beneath the arches of the Procuratie.

'Do you come to Venice often?' asked the President.

'I hadn't been since my honeymoon, but I've come back now with my wife and son.'

'You are right to come back. I come whenever I can.'

'Yesterday, we climbed to the top of the Bovolo,' said Daniel.

'You are a man of taste, Monsieur Mercier. The Campanile is for tourists, but only those who truly love

Venice climb the Bovolo. There's a beautiful cloister just near here, too, the only example of Romanesque art in Venice. Very few people know it. I will show you on our way out.'

'Thank you,' murmured Daniel.

'When I think that there are people who say Venice is a melancholy place ...' the head of state went on, blinking.

'I'm not one of them,' said Daniel. 'For me, Venice is uplifting ... and Venice is beauty.'

'Yes, beauty ...' agreed François Mitterrand.

Daniel was living his reward, right here, right now. Beyond any material recompense, his wish, his dream, his heart's desire had been granted.

He had become the fourth guest at the President's table.

Epilogue

The black-and-white photograph was so beautifully printed it could almost have been a Cartier-Bresson. The picture showed Daniel Mercier on his way out of the SOGETEC building, the black felt hat on his head. The man in the grey tie looked intently at his colleague, before turning to the President.

'We can get it back, Monsieur le Président.'

'How do you plan to go about it?' asked the head of state, from behind his spectacles.

'We overpower him in the street and take it back.'

'No!' exclaimed François Mitterrand. 'No violence. He'd guess straight away that I was behind it ... No,' he repeated softly, and sank into one of his frequent, disconcerting silences. 'Follow it.'

'"It", Monsieur le Président?'

'The hat, of course.'

And the man in the grey tie left the office accompanied by his colleague.

An hour after the President had left his hat in the

brasserie, two of his security officers had gone back to collect it. The hat was no longer there. It was a clear case of theft. The head waiter confirmed that the man at the table next to the President's had left wearing a black felt hat. Had he been wearing it when he came in? Confused and embarrassed, the head waiter confessed that he could not be sure. The man was not a regular customer, he hadn't booked, and had paid by Carte Bleue. The men from the Élysée left with a copy of the receipt. Daniel Mercier was located the very next day.

When Daniel left the hat on the train, a telex arrived on the Élysée's private line that same evening, announcing that it had been picked up by a blonde woman. The following morning, François Mitterrand, who never slept at the Élysée, read the message over coffee.

'How interesting,' he said. 'A woman? Do we have a picture?'

Later that day, a photograph of Fanny Marquant in Parc Monceau landed on the President's desk, with an accompanying note: 'The woman left the hat on a bench; the man who picked it up is currently being investigated.'

'Why did she leave it on the bench?'

'I don't know, Monsieur le Président. We're looking into every possible explanation,' replied the man in the grey tie.

'She's a very attractive woman,' observed the head of state before handing back the photograph.

When Daniel's notice appeared in the newspaper, it was immediately picked up. Élysée security officers asked the newspaper for a copy of every letter received in response, in the interests of national security.

And so, on a sunny afternoon in the grounds of the Élysée Palace, the President was able to read Fanny Marquant's short story 'The Hat'.

Some time later, when he learnt that the perfumer Aslan had launched a new fragrance, François Mitterrand had his people get hold of a bottle.

When the men from the Élysée learnt from one of the letters that Aslan no longer had the hat, the news provoked a flurry of anxiety that lasted several hours. How could he no longer have it when he had been wearing it on his way home just the previous day?

For several weeks, the man in the grey tie studiously avoided the subject with the head of state. Then came Aslan's more detailed letter about the loss of the hat.

Two men were immediately despatched to the brasserie. Armed with fake tax-office identity cards, they pored over the accounts and identified Bernard Lavallière, who had paid by cheque, as the new wearer of the hat. The resulting surveillance operation was centred on Rue de Passy.

'The perfumer no longer has the hat? And you hadn't noticed …'

'No, Monsieur le Président. There was something of a mix-up.'

'How very vexing,' said the head of state tightly. 'Who is this Lavallière?' he added.

'A man from AXA. There's a dossier on its way, Monsieur le Président.'

Some time later the man in the grey tie came to find

the President at the bottom of the Élysée Palace garden, where he was throwing sticks for his black labrador.

'Mercier has stolen it,' he announced.

'Indeed? He really is a very resourceful chap.'

That same afternoon, François Mitterrand asked for the Librairie de la Mouette to be added to the list of bookshops supplying the Élysée.

'There are no new developments in the case of the hat, Monsieur le Président,' said the man in the grey tie one day, during a review of the President's private files. 'Should we continue to have it followed?'

'No,' said the head of state, after a moment's thought. 'Let destiny take its course,' he added meditatively.

'Destroy or archive, Monsieur le Président?'

'Destroy, of course.'

The next day, the man in the grey tie returned to the President's office with the hat dossier under his arm. François Mitterrand put on his glasses, leafed through the reports and photographs one last time, and paused to look at the picture of Fanny Marquant sitting in Parc Monceau with his hat on her head. He removed it from the file and put it to one side.

'Personal archives,' he said.

Then he initialled the order to destroy the rest.

Twenty years later, on 29 January 2008, François Mitterrand's private effects were sold at auction, at Paris's Hôtel Drouot.

The 369 lots included his suits, ties and shirts, personal gifts from foreign heads of state, and no fewer than nineteen hats: five felt hats, two woollen hats, one in suede, two top hats, a bowler, and eight straw boaters.

The black Homburg bought by the French Socialist Party that day may or may not have been the hat in this story. Every hat-wearer's life is measured in a succession of headgear that wears out, is mislaid and found, or sometimes never seen again.

The fact that this was the only black hat in the sale is curious indeed: did he have others? Probably. Did his relatives hold on to them? Quite possibly. We will never know.

And as the hammer fell on each lot, Pierre Aslan was sipping a glass of Asti across the square from the Uffizi Palace in Florence. After his dazzling return to the international scene, he created no further fragrances. It was a deliberate decision.

He preferred to bow out on a high note and focus on building his personal legend. Some sources claim he went on concocting perfumes in secret for private clients, charging a small fortune for his services. The Sultan of Brunei and even Bill Gates were among the names mentioned, but this was never confirmed.

Pierre Aslan moved to Florence where he still lives today, out of the public eye. He has granted no interviews since 1987.

Fanny Marquant's lover Édouard Lanier continued to cheat on his wife, who asked for a divorce in 1992. He remarried a much younger woman, who cheated on him in turn, then left him. After retiring from his post at Danone, he invested his money in a chain of massage parlours in Thailand, where he lived with a woman named Bongkoj.

He has been missing since the tsunami of 2004.

Dr Fremenberg died silently in his consulting room one day in 2001, in the middle of a therapy session. His African art collection was sold at Christie's in 2002 as the 'Collection of Dr F.'.

The statuette with the erect penis that Aslan had so disliked was auctioned for 120,500 euros including costs. It is now in a private collection in Washington.

Esther Kerwitcz carried on touring until 2000, after which she decided to end her concert career and made just four final recordings. Known to music lovers today as the 'Tetra Kerwitcz', they are some of the most downloaded classical performances on the web. She lives in Florence with Pierre Aslan.

Fanny Marquant became the widow of Michel Carlier – the man in the grey hat – a few years after opening her bookshop.

She ran the business for another fifteen years and had many lovers, until a British lord fell madly in love with her during a holiday on the Normandy coast. He married her and took her to Sussex, where Fanny was extremely bored.

She has still not mastered the English language. Her short novel *The French Lady* was a critical success, with enthusiastic reviews in the British press and an author interview in the *Daily Mirror*. She still thinks of Michel Carlier as the love of her life.

Bernard Lavallière became an even more passionate admirer of Jean-Michel Basquiat, whom he met briefly one morning in January 1988 when, by chance, the artist was not completely drunk or stoned, and was not the least offended by the man in the three-piece suit and tie who spoke with such sincerity about the vibrations of his canvases.

By the time of the artist's death, seven months later, Lavallière owned no fewer than nine of his paintings, including five from his finest period (1981–3). In the years that followed, Bernard continued to buy more, until the American's works began fetching prices beyond his means.

And when the canvases he had bought for 150,000 or 200,000 francs soared in value to 10 million dollars each in 2010, the derision of his peers turned to horrified fascination and sheer hatred.

Daniel Mercier retired to the Pays d'Auge. He ended his career as head of SOGETEC Normandy. To amuse himself, he has secretly begun writing an account of his adventure with the President's hat. He's written twenty pages and he's only just getting started.

He still cannot eat oysters and vinegar without hearing the words 'As I was saying to Helmut Kohl last week'.

A few months after recovering his hat, François Mitterrand shattered the pollsters' predictions and was re-elected with 54.2 per cent of the vote. Weakened by illness, he spent his last Christmas at Aswan, in Egypt, before returning suddenly to France, where he died a week later, during the winter of 1996.

He bowed out of the presidency leaving a final enigma for the nation: during his last New Year address to the French people, he uttered a curious phrase that seemed out of place amongst the usual conventions.

Much has been said about it, but no one has given a satisfactory interpretation of its meaning. He himself never explained it. Even today, the phrase scores millions of hits on Google.

Twenty-three seconds from the end of his address on 31 December 1994, the President looked straight into the camera: 'I believe in the power of the spirit and I will never leave you.'

Daniel Mercier voiced by Louise Rogers Lalaurie

Fanny Marquant and Bernard Lavallière
voiced by Emily Boyce

Pierre Aslan voiced by Jane Aitken

Reading Group Questions

- Daniel Mercier is overwhelmed to be in possession of François Mitterrand's hat. Why have the iconic belongings of the famous always held such a fascination?

- François Mitterrand worked hard as a young man to overcome his inherent shyness. What do you think the book tells us about self-confidence?

- Daniel Mercier, Fanny Marquant, Pierre Aslan and Bernard Lavallière: which one of them makes the most significant life change whilst owning the hat?

- Why do you think Antoine Laurain chose these four particular temporary custodians of the hat through which to tell his story?

- How does François Mitterrand come across in the novel?

- The hat is described as a beautiful, lustrous, stylish item. Given the chance, would you have taken it and, if so, why?

- Apart from the references to technology and contemporary culture, what more does the book tell us about how life has changed since the 1980s?

- How is love depicted in the story?

- The book is light-hearted and pacy. How does the author ensure that the narrative keeps moving along?

- It was the magic of the hat that made the characters change their lives – or was it? Having read the book, what do you think?

Interview with Antoine Laurain

Where did the idea for The President's Hat *come from?*
Possibly from losing my own hat! It happened a few years ago. The next morning, I went back to the café where I had left it and – it was nowhere to be seen. No one had handed it in. So my disappointment was coupled with a disconcerting realisation: that all the while I was trying to retrieve my hat, someone else in some other part of the city was wearing it. I hope it was a woman who did the deed, and that she's pretty ...

What made you decide to set your story in the 1980s?
I wanted to go back to my childhood and teenage years; the days before the internet, mobile phones, iPods and iPads and rap music, when there were only six TV channels to choose from. It's the very recent past, but it feels like another age. The world has moved at an astonishing pace since the year 2000. Everything is happening so quickly – too quickly – and it's speeding up all the time. I felt the need to take a step back. Judging by how well the book has been received, I wasn't the only one.

The President is an iconic figure in the novel. Are you an admirer of Mitterrand, the man?
It's difficult to imagine how anyone who was in France in the eighties could have failed to be impressed by the figure

of Mitterrand, whatever their political persuasion: his noble profile; sphinx-like silences; political manoeuvres worthy of a Florentine prince; his voice and, not least, his hat. He belongs to a breed of politician we will never see again. But remember this isn't a political novel, rather, it should be read like a kind of fable. The President only appears at the beginning and end of the book.

There are other real-life characters and actual events featured in the novel. Do you enjoy mixing the fictional and the real?
Very much. It's a fundamental part of creative writing and especially so in the case of *The President's Hat*. Some readers have even asked me if it was a true story! Perhaps it really did happen, without anyone knowing.

Your novel came out in France on the eve of the presidential elections in which François Hollande became the second socialist President of the Republic, following Mitterrand. How has French politics changed between the two presidencies?
Much has changed, not least the ways in which politicians present themselves to the public and their relationships with the media, but that's not particular to France. What strikes me most is that it's becoming less and less common to find political figures who stand out from the crowd.

In the UK you had Margaret Thatcher, a very strong personality, who made a real impression on people in other countries. A true character. I remember coming to stay near Oxford for a language trip in '86 or '87 and the first thing the father of my host family said when I arrived was, 'You're so lucky to have Mitterrand in France,' before

adding mournfully, 'We've got Margaret Thatcher ...'
A few months later, I was reading an article in a French
newspaper arguing that what we in France really needed
was someone like ... Margaret Thatcher!

Whatever you think of their politics, there's no doubt
the two of them were huge personalities.

*The story takes place in a world in which people communicate
via Minitel; Canal +, answerphones and CDs are novelties.
What impact do you think technology has on our lives today?*
Technology has a lot going for it. For one thing, it means
I can reply to these questions by email; I could even take
a photo of the cat asleep on my lap and send it to you in
less than a minute – something which would have been
inconceivable not long ago.

That said, I'm wary of technology's apparently endless
onward march. I preferred vinyl to virtual downloads and
I very much hope the physical book continues to exist.

*Destiny and magic play an important role in the plot ... do you
believe in them?*
Certainly the former and quite possibly the latter. I'm
going to take the liberty of quoting Vladimir Nabokov,
whose words on the subject far exceed anything I might
have to say. It comes from one of his lectures on literature
given in the USA: 'The truth is that great novels are great
fairy tales ... literature was born on the day when a boy
came crying "wolf, wolf" and there was no wolf behind
him.'

You're a film-maker and antiques collector as well as a novelist. How do these other activities influence your writing? My scriptwriting work has helped with the construction of my novels. You, the reader, should be carried seamlessly through the story with the impression of everything just flowing along naturally. In fact, it has all been constructed as carefully and painstakingly as a Rolls-Royce engine.

As for my collecting, that mostly influences my bank balance! Although my passion for objects, auctions and dealers did provide the material for my first novel, published in 2007 and entitled *Ailleurs si j'y suis*, which was the story of a collector. By a strange twist of fate, it was awarded the Prix Drouot, the literary prize founded by the famous Paris auction house.

Which authors have had the greatest effect on you?
There are so many writers I admire: Sacha Guitry, Céline and Modiano to name just a few. I'm a big fan of British detective fiction, which has also taught me a lot about the construction of novels. Not to mention cinema and the great film-makers like Billy Wilder and Lubitsch. I'd also include Somerset Maugham's short stories, which are astonishing and have hardly aged at all. And I recently discovered P. G. Wodehouse's Jeeves series – brilliant!

What's the nicest thing anyone has said to you about The President's Hat?
'If only I had a president's hat of my own!' That's something I've heard several times at book signings. It means that reading this optimistic novel has made people happy, which is praise enough for me.